One Love
Two Wives

By Janette Grant

Mindworks Publishing

Mindworks Publishing
Copyright © 2021 by Mindworks Publishing
Published by Mindworks Publishing,
Missouri City, TX 77489

Cover Design: Mindworks Publishing

. . . and seek help from Allah and do not lose heart, and if anything (in the form of trouble) comes to you, don't say: If I had not done that, it would not have happened so and so, but say: Allah did what He had ordained to do . . .

Book 33, Number 6441
Kitab Ul Qadr
Sahih Muslim

Chapter One

Springtime

Springtime. My favorite time of the year. The time of year when everything is fresh and new; when the earth is being reborn from the slumber of winter; when even the air we breathe feels renewed by the promise of beginnings. Today the sun is bright, the breeze is cool, and I can smell the sweetness of lilacs in the air.

Gabriel is sleeping soundly in his stroller after walking a couple of laps around the running track at the park behind Hope High School, and I'm feeling like I might have actually burned away a few more pounds after that walk. The heat of the early afternoon sun warms my cheeks and I'm reluctant to leave the park, but if I hurry home, I'll have a few free hours to eat something and to read a little before he wakes up.

I get a couple of sideways looks as I exit the park, not because of my baggy grey sweatpants and oversized white t-shirt, but because of the light grey headscarf tied around my head. I smile cordially as I pass and keep it moving.

The nice weather has drawn people out today so there's a diverse mix of college students, people from the surrounding neighborhood, and kids sprinkled throughout the park, and I never get a second look from that crowd, but the two women sitting on a bench in the little playground I just passed seem to have an opinion about my scarf. Most of our neighbors are African American or Cape Verdean families, and predominantly Christian, so Islam is foreign to them, other than what they may see on the news or in television programs.

Walking slowly, I leave the park and start heading back to my parents' house. I pass Olney Street Baptist Church, where the parking lot is filled with cars of people that have arrived for Saturday Service, and then I walk past my old elementary school where the sidewalks are cracked, but clean, and much smaller and narrower than I remember them being when I was little.

I reach my street and turn to walk the short distance to our driveway. The lady who lives across the street eyes me and my headscarf suspiciously as I push the stroller past her and towards my parent's little green and white house. I don't know her name, but my mother says she's nosy. I offer her a smile, but she turns away quickly.

It's been about a month since I'd taken my shahadah and converted to Islam, so these kinds of responses are relatively new and I try not to let them bother me too much, mainly because I'm beginning to understand how difficult it is for people in the neighborhood who don't know anything about Islam to trust that it isn't a foreign religion that worships a different God. My strategy is to show them the benefits of Islam and the similarities between Islam and Christianity by my example. After all, most of my family is

Christian so my love for them makes it easy for me to seek common ground.

It had been hard for my parents to accept my conversion to Islam at first but once they realized that I hadn't started worshipping a different God, and that Christianity and Islam has a lot in common, they were able to relax. They had worked hard to put me and my siblings through Catholic school and although they only attend church infrequently and on holidays, they are staunchly "in Jesus' name" Christians. Besides the fact that it was hard for my mother to reign herself in about Christmas and my not celebrating Christian holidays anymore, we've been able to compromise, and she has even begun to ask me about the Islamic holidays.

I push the stroller up the driveway and past the backyard to the back-door entrance where I unlock the door and enter quietly so I don't wake up Gabriel. Everyone is out today so it's just me and him, my Gabey. I carefully maneuver the stroller through the narrow hallway, making sure not to bump into the coat rack.

I think my parents said earlier that they were spending the day at my grandmother's house, and my Aunt Pam, who lives in the guest bedroom, has gone on a day trip with her book club somewhere. My younger brother James and my baby sister Jasmine are out with their friends, and Michael, my husband, didn't come back to Rhode Island this weekend.

I carefully lift Gabriel from the stroller and cross the kitchen to the living room at the front of the house so I can remove his little hat and jacket to lay him down in the basinet that we keep in the living room for nap times. He squirms and fusses a little but soon goes back to sleep. I smooth down the silky black curls of his hair, the same color as mine, but softer and finer, and kiss his little brown cheek before stepping away.

With a quiet sigh of relief, I remove my headscarf and kick off my sneakers before plopping down onto the couch to take a minute to myself. My own thick black curls are slicked back into a tight bun at the nape of my neck, so I loosen my scrunchie to let my hair out and rub my scalp.

Saturdays are usually filled with chores and getting ready for the work week ahead, but my mother had done the grocery shopping this week, and Michael hadn't come home so I didn't have much laundry to do. My thoughts drift to the book I'd bought recently, about the history of Islam in Africa, and I'm about to get up to go find it when the phone rings. I jump up quickly from the couch to answer it so the sound doesn't wake Gabey.

"Hello," I say when I reach the end table beside the love seat and pick up the receiver.

"Hey, it's me. As salaamu alaikum," Michael replies.

My heart skips a beat. We've been married for over two years and it still does that.

"Walaikum as salaam," I respond, and I can't help but smile. "How's everything? Are you getting a lot done?"

He had said that he couldn't come home this weekend because he had to work and to study for an exam on Monday, so this is a surprise. The final semester of his senior year of college is upon him and he commutes back and forth between Massachusetts and Rhode Island to save money. It's cheaper for me to live here with my parents than in married student housing on campus, so here I am, excited at his call and hoping that he's eating well, getting enough sleep at night, and able to talk for a little while.

"Everything is good. I actually got a lot done at the library, and Dr. Qadhi said that I could take the rest of today and tomorrow off so I'm going to come back for the night and study there. I'll have to leave tomorrow night to get back for the exam, but I miss my baby and I want to come home," he says warmly.

His side job, in addition to his work study job at the university's Religious Studies Department's library, is at one of the local mosques in Boston working as an intern to the Imam. The position includes everything from coffee runs for the other staff members, to organizing entire fundraising events. Ironically, the mosque has recently completed construction for adding a wing to the building for a library, so he's been on library duty at both jobs.

"I miss you too," I reply as I sit down onto the love seat, smiling even wider and twirling the telephone cord around my finger, subconsciously responding to the possibility of seeing him soon. "Have the bookshelves gotten there yet? That won't be too much back and forth for you if you come tonight, I hope? I don't want you to come all the way back if it's easier for you to stay there."

That is only partially true, because I really do want him to come all the way home, but I also want him to take care of himself. He takes the T back and forth between Rhode Island and Massachusetts every weekend, and the ride isn't that long, but I know that it's tiring and that he hardly eats anything other than fast food when he's away. I don't want to make things more difficult for him.

Married life has been challenging for both of us, and the pressures of the past year since Gabriel had been born were taking a toll on our relationship despite our efforts and commitment. As college students, we had been bright eyed and optimistic about everything. We hadn't hesitated to jump into marriage when we'd realized that we wanted to be together, but living together, witnessing each other's faults and having to pay bills has a sobering effect.

When we'd met during my freshman year of college and his sophomore year, the connection had been immediate and intense. We had spent almost all of our free time together after that first meeting, and before long, we were exclusively dating and making plans for the future. We were engaged by my sophomore year and then I got pregnant. Needless to say, that changed our trajectory. The decisions that were required of us from that moment forward had added a pressure that had almost suffocated the relationship. Thankfully, since converting to Islam, things had been improving.

"Yes, they came earlier this week, so we've been labelling books and transferring them to the shelves every day," he says tiredly before continuing. "But it's fine. I'm good, and I want to talk to you about something anyway. I don't want to talk about it over the phone."

I sense a tension in his voice all of sudden and I wonder about it in the back of mind, but I say, "Ok. Well, I'm glad that you're coming home, even if it's only for one night. Gabey just mastered climbing up the stairs by himself. Aunt Pam said that she has to make sure that the gate stays up all the time, so she doesn't lose sight of him."

Talking about Gabriel and his developments is always a safe space for us, especially if one of us is tense or anxious about something.

I can hear the smile in Michael's voice when he replies, "My boy. It's amazing how much he grows from week to week. What's he doing now?"

"Sleeping," I tell him candidly. "I took him for a walk in the stroller to the park a little while ago. He was fussy and fighting his nap, and it's nice out today so I figured I'd take him out, but he fell asleep while I was walking the track, so he didn't even get to play in the playground!"

We laugh together, familiar with Gabey's stubborn resistance to napping and his susceptibility to a cool breeze and steady motion – it's his personal kryptonite. Michael's

13

laugh washes over me and even through the phone I can feel the warmth. I want to ask him what he wants to talk about, but since he'd already said that he'd rather talk in person I bit my tongue and tried to be patient. It is hard, though, and that is definitely the journalism training in me. He jokingly calls me Barbara Walters because I tend to subconsciously question him so much, and I always want to know the who, what, when, where and how of a situation.

"I can't wait to see him. And you. I'm going to check the train schedule now and head back to the apartment so I can pack a bag and get going," he says.

"Ok," I reply, and I can hear voices in the background. "Are you still at the mosque?"

"Yeah," he says distractedly and offers salaams to someone who must have come near him. "I just wanted to call and make sure that you were home. I'll be there in a few hours."

"Ok. I love you. As salaamu alaikum," I say, hearing an increase in the volume of the background voices.

"I love you too, wasalaamu alaikum," he says lowly, as if not wanting to be overheard, and he hangs up.

He's never hung up that way before, but it's Saturday, and the mosque is often busy on the weekends. I try to dismiss it, but there's a nagging, persistent curiosity tugging at my mind. I hang up the phone and do my best to categorize it as my nosy, journalistic tendencies and I go to find my book so I can get some reading done. I will know soon enough what he wants to talk about.

"Take it easy, Joanna," I tell myself as I walk over to the dining room table.

I'd placed some of my books and study notebooks there last night and that's exactly where I find the thick volume that I'm looking for. I had left it beside my Arabic language workbook and some of Michael's books that are also stacked up on the table. Books are our thing. And as nerdy as it feels to think about it, some of our best dates have been spent browsing in, and shopping at bookstores for hours.

I go back into the living room and sit down on the couch with my back against one of the arms and with my legs stretched out in front of me. A quick glance over at the basinet less than a foot away from me lets me know that Gabriel is still sleeping soundly so I open up the book to my bookmarked page and start reading, but Michael isn't far from my thoughts.

Chapter Two

The Announcement

I am stunned. Completely and deeply stunned. Paralyzed. All I can do is stare at him as tears roll down my face. This can't be real.

"Jo?" Michael asks gently, shaking my shoulder lightly. "You heard me, right? Are you ok?"

"Am I ok?" I repeat hysterically in my head as his voice pulls me back to reality. "Hell, no, I'm not ok!!!"

That's what I think, but I don't say anything out loud. I can't. I simply can't form words. The tears roll more heavily down my face, covering my cheeks and streaming down my neck. I open my mouth to speak but a sob catches in my throat, so I quickly close it again. I glance over at Gabriel where he sits on the rug playing with his toys and I try feebly to pull myself together. I cannot break down. I will not break down, especially not in front of the baby. I grasp desperately onto my faith, searching my mind for a comforting scripture – for a word to strengthen me in the face of this.

I have nothing. No deep, inspiring wisdom comes to my mind, so I offer an instinctive, primal prayer: *please, God, help me through this.* I close my eyes and a miraculous, supernatural calm comes over me.

It's Sunday evening and we'd had an early dinner, just the two of us, at my favorite Indian restaurant. We hadn't had a real date in over a year, so I'd worn my favorite light green abaya and matching headscarf and he'd actually worn a shirt and tie. It was the nicest time that we'd had together in a long while. We talked to each other and about each other, and about how things are going in our jobs, and about the baby and his growth rather than about bills or how to earn more money to pay bills.

We'd just gotten back home less than twenty minutes ago and when he'd sat me down on the bed, holding my hand and telling me that he wanted to talk to me about something, his eyes had sparkled, and I had known that he was happy – I'd thought he had some romantic surprise for me. This was not that. At all.

I wipe my face with my palms and slowly look up at my husband. My Michael. Well, not just my Michael anymore. Tears sting my eyes anew, but I blink them away this time, taking a deep calming breath and preparing my mind and heart to speak. It is difficult. Sooo difficult. But I summon the courage and the composure to respond.

"Yes. I heard you," I say, but my voice breaks with emotion and I have to blink back tears again.

We sit there in silence, staring at each other. His light brown eyes are filled with compassion, but I can see his resolve. He had really done it and I felt helpless and broken-hearted. He's seated next to me on our bed with his hand lightly on my shoulder, and he reaches over to wipe away the remaining wetness from my cheek. I sigh sadly and close my eyes at his touch, but I will not let myself cry anymore. Not now. Not in front of him and the baby. I will wait until I can lock myself in the bathroom later and then cry my heart out. Anger and my own stony resolve gradually kick in. I open my eyes and scoot away from him on the bed, putting some space between us.

His eyes widen a little with surprise at the movement, but he lets his hand fall to the mattress between us without responding. The baby toddles over to us and smiling, grabs onto the edge of the mattress to get our attention. His smile and dimples fill his little face and squints his eyes, just like his dad. Once he's balanced himself, he lets go of the mattress and claps his hands, looking between the two of us, and expecting us to follow his lead and to clap along with him, as we always do when he accomplishes something.

I smile down at him, my eyes filling with tears that I can't blink away this time, and I reach over to pick him up. His soft little arms wrap around my neck and he lays his head on my shoulder.

"Mama. Mama. Mama," he repeats in his sweet little voice before yawning widely.

I stand up from the bed with him in my arms and turn to face Michael.

"The baby's tired. I'm going to go put him down for a nap," I say as nicely as I can.

Michael frowns slightly and says, "But are you ok? Are we going to talk about this?"

Anger flares in my mind at that. Now he wants to talk. After he had already married a second wife. After the deed has been done. After he had taken me out and softened me up and had made me feel as if I am the most important person in his life. Dozens of angry remarks come to my mind but the squirming baby in my arms keeps me in check.

"No, I'm not ok," I say, my voice raising slightly before I can compose myself, but compose myself I do. "I don't want to talk to you right now. And honestly, I don't even know what to say. Like you said, 'you have a right to take on another wife.' I wish you would have talked to me about it first but-"

He cuts me off and interrupts me to respond heatedly, "I did! I told you about this many times-"

It's my turn to interrupt him and I reply angrily, "Told me is not talking to me about it! I should have had some say in this. And now I don't want to talk to *you* about it. I'm going to put the baby to sleep."

I turn abruptly on my heel and walk over to the rocking chair beside Gabriel's crib. My heart races in my chest and the baby lifts his little head to look up at me, as if sensing the turmoil inside of me. I kiss his little cheeks and sit down in the rocking chair to nurse him.

He latches on immediately and painfully, his tiny teeth scratching against my skin, and closes his eyes. I gently rock him back and forth, subconsciously noting that I will have to start weaning him soon, and I close my eyes too.

Michael remains there on the bed, frowning and fuming inside because I had walked away from him, but he makes no move to continue the conversation. After a few minutes of sitting in silence, he gets up and goes to the bathroom to make wudu.

I sigh with relief when he's gone, but I can't ignore the quiet emptiness and the regret I feel for reacting the way that I have. We never argue like this. We get into tense disagreements sometimes, but we've never raised our voices at each other this way. I can feel a gulf forming between us, and waves of anger and frustration pushing us apart. I can't talk to him right now, though. I feel too much hurt, too much betrayal, too much anger.

Tears fill my eyes and roll down my cheeks, but I quickly wipe them away and look down at my child. He is almost asleep, his little jaws barely moving, and his tiny fist clutching onto the fabric of my abaya. I smooth down the curls of his hair and hum his favorite song.

"You are my sunshine. My only sunshine. You make me happy when skies are gray. You'll never know dear; how much I love you. Please don't take my sunshine away."

Michael comes out of the bathroom and walks over to the prayer area set up across from our bed. That side of the carpeted and refurbished space is on the side of the basement that is considered our "living room." He begins to offer salaat, and as much as I want to shout and to rant and rave at him, seeing him standing there, turning to God and praying instead of trying to force me to have a conversation with him, reminds me of the love we share. I close my eyes, trying to block out the image of him so that I can hold onto the resentment that I'm feeling, but I can't.

The anger is drowned out by the sadness welling beneath it and I don't fight the tears as they flow fast and hot down my face. Gabriel drifts off to sleep in my arms and the sun begins its decline through the windows, dimming the light in a way that reflects the diminishing of my spirit.

Chapter Three

The Aftermath

Late afternoon sunlight paints the sky bright pink and orange as my mother and I drive home from work a few days later. I stare through the passenger window at the passing cars, seeing, but not seeing.

"He's a good man, Jo. Don't be too hasty. It's hard to find a good man," my mother says matter-of-factly as she steers the car around a corner and onto Thayer Street.

My mother has a way of making things plain when I need to hear it most. Having had me when she was young, our friendship is just as strong and loving as our mother-daughter relationship is. Her soft features reflect her thoughtfulness as she responds to my telling her about plural marriage and Michael's decision.

It's been almost a week since Michael announced that he had married a second wife and it had been the worst week of my life. He'd gone back to Boston Sunday night after he'd told me, and although I was glad to have some time to myself, I had hardly slept or eaten all week long. I hadn't told anyone yet about this, just my mom.

"He's back at school now, right?" my mother asks as we reach a traffic light just as it turns red, forcing the car to come to a stop.

A group of college students, all of them wearing shorts and sweatshirts, stroll past the front of the car leisurely while we wait.

"Yeah," I say, blinking away the tears that form at her question and wishing that I felt as carefree as those college students looked.

I wished also, more than ever, that I could be there in Boston with Michael, but I'd decided to take a leave of absence from college to work and to take care of the baby. So here I sit, driving home from work with my mother, instead of being in Boston with my husband. I sigh dejectedly, regretting my decision to stay in Rhode Island.

Fortunately, my parents had the furnished basement so I had moved in with them while Michael worked and went to school, and I'd thought it would be smart to stay with my parents so I'd have help with Gabriel, but I would have chosen to apply for married housing if I'd known Michael would end up taking a second wife. Yes, Michael is a good man, but is that enough for me to consider staying in this marriage?

"And this is ok in Islam, right? It's not like he's cheating on you or anything?" my mother asks when the light turns green.

She turns onto Hope Street and we drive away from the university campus where we work.

"Yeah," I reply again, disheartened anew.

My mother is right: in Islam the husband can take up to four wives as long as he is able to take care of them emotionally and financially with equality. I hadn't known that when I'd taken shahadah, but I don't think that would have stopped me. Learning about Islam has been my saving grace, and I have only gotten through the past work week because I've been reading the Quran, and because I have my daily salaat and dua to lean on.

"Families in Africa practice polygamy all of the time; and some of the indigenous tribes in South America too," my mother says diplomatically. "Maybe it's because I'm older now, but I wouldn't object to having another woman around to help with the cooking and the cleaning; and with taking care of the kids."

I continue to stare out the window as she drives and reply, "Yeah. I know."

But in my mind, I think, *"You've been working in the African American Studies Department for too long."*

But again, she isn't wrong. I can relate to the possibility of having another woman around to help with home-making responsibilities, but I shudder at the thought of kids. That means Michael will have to create those kids with someone besides me! I can't even imagine being able to accept that.

"And think about our community? Indigenous tribes have been practicing polygamy for centuries and they are still thriving," my mother continues, her brown eyes bright with enthusiasm. "Too many black children don't know who their fathers are. If women were given the chance to stay in committed relationships with their children's fathers, it could make a real difference in our communities. I don't see polygamy as something negative in and of itself, honey. Do you?"

I sigh, unable to rationally disagree with her and answer, "No."

Because the truth of the matter is that I don't think polygyny is bad, I just don't want it for myself. If someone else wants to jump on board and share her husband with other women, may God grant her ease, but I don't want to. And I can rationalize how some black nationalist notions of plural marriage for the sake of community, and how traditional African practices might cure many of the challenges facing African Americans here in the U.S., but it doesn't take away the hurt. Or the jealousy.

"What's with the short answers?" my mother asks, only half-jokingly. "I thought you wanted to talk to me about this?"

She's one of those mothers who feel her children's pain more deeply than they do so I know she's trying to make me feel better.

I take a deep breath and respond, "I just don't know what to do. I love the religion of Islam, and I love Michael so much, but I don't want this. I don't want to share him with another woman."

Uttering the words aloud release the flood gates, and the pain from the truth of that statement come crashing over me. I sob like the world is ending, gasping for breath and holding my face in my hands so my mother won't see my face. In my oblivion I notice that she has stopped the car and has pulled over so she can hug me.

She unbuckles her seatbelt and wraps her arms around me, patting my back, and letting my tears soak into her sweater, but she doesn't say a word. She just lets me cry. Occasionally, she whispers, "my baby" against my headscarf, but other than that, she just holds onto me, anchoring me, as I'm tossed by the storm of my aching heart.

When I'm finally spent and feeling like I've been squeezed and wrung out like a sponge, she kisses my cheek and looks me in the eyes until I manage a smile.

She smiles widely and wisely in response and says, "If you were a drinker, I'd say let's go have some wine. But you're going to be just fine. The decision is up to you. You know that, but make sure you think it through all the way before you choose. I'll support you no matter what. And I'm not going to tell your father for now. I'll let you tell him this one."

She had been the one to tell my dad about my conversion to Islam and that hadn't gone well at all. We both laugh, imagining my extremely over-protective father's response, but in the back of my mind I know that it is going to be an even harder sell to tell him about plural marriage than it was about Islam.

And in that moment, I realize that deep down, I have already decided. Even with the crying and the lack of sleep I know that I'm not going to leave Michael. I'm going to tough it out and see where this experience will lead me. When I think about it further, I realize that I have enough faith to consider that if God permits it, there has to be good in it. And maybe, if I just can't handle the idea of sharing my husband, I'll change my mind and decide to leave later. For now, in my heart, I have accepted the fact that I have become a first wife.

My mother kisses my cheek one more time and starts up the car.

"So, have you met her yet? Who is she, this second wife?" my mother asks curiously now that she is sure that I'm not going to break down into tears again.

I blink, startled by her question. I hadn't even thought about the "who" in this situation, I'd been too tossed around by the "what." And the fact of the matter is that I don't know. Michael and I hadn't gotten around to that part of the discussion when he'd made his announcement. I had hardly been able to accept his saying, "I've taken a second wife," never mind having to hear her name or to see his face when he spoke about her. Speculating about it now makes my heart pick up its pace with anxiety.

"I don't know yet," I respond, and I try to keep the worry out of my voice. "We didn't get past him telling me that he had already married her, and I haven't spoken to him since he left Sunday night."

My mother becomes quiet and pensive, as if she has her own suspicions, but she doesn't say anything else. My mother has the mixed ethnicity of African American, Native American and Cape Verdean heritage, and the wise-woman, matriarchal roots of our traditions dominate her expression as lifts an eyebrow and her face shifts into a look of doubtful, wary anticipation. I can tell that she sees this variable as a possible problem for me.

"Well, make sure you're ready to hear whatever he has to say on that front, honey," she says, cautioning me in the way that only she can because she knows me so well.

I don't get angry or upset often, but because of that very reason, everyone in our family knows to watch out if I do. And I get that not only from my mama, but my daddy has a bit of a temper too if poked in the wrong way.

"I will, mom," I say, but inside I'm not so sure if I can be patient enough to hear Michael out about this.

We drive the rest of the way home in a comfortable silence, but the gears of my mind have been set in motion. Who was this woman who had eased her way into his heart and into our marriage? I think back to when he had taken me to the Cranston Street mosque to make my shahadah and I try to remember if I had seen any women paying undue attention to him there. Then I think about Boston and the mosque that he attends and works at, and the possibility of him having met someone at jumuah prayer or at an Islamic event or lecture.

Anger rears its head again as these thoughts float through my mind. How could he? How could he have possibly married another woman without talking to me about it first? Without introducing her to me to make sure that we would get along? Without giving me the chance to say, I don't want this?

By the time we turn into our driveway I am fuming inside and I'm ready for an argument. I check my watch for the time to make sure that he will be out of class and not at work if I call him. According to his schedule, he should be out class by now and on his way back to the apartment that he shares with his best friend. He has fifteen minutes to get ready to hear it from me.

I slam the car door a little too hard and get a surprised, sideways look from my mother.

"Sorry," I say, but my mind is preoccupied with rehearsing what I'm going to say when I speak to him.

My mother unlocks the back door, and we enter into the hallway to take off our jackets and to hang them up on the coat rack before going into the kitchen. My younger sister Jasmine is at the kitchen table feeding Gabriel, and my Aunt Pam, who watches Gabriel for me during the day while I'm at work, stands at the sink washing the dishes.

"Hey family," Aunt Pam calls out over her shoulder with a wide smile, her round face and almond-shaped light brown eyes shining with her usual good humor. "How goes it ladies?"

"Hey, sis," my mom replies to my aunt before walking over to the table to kiss Gabey first and then my sister on the top of her head. "Hey, my baby, how was school?"

"Hey Auntie, hey Jaz," I reply, trying to sound like I'm not fuming inside.

"It was good," my sister says to my mom and spoons another mouthful of applesauce into Gabey's open mouth.

At fifteen my sister looks so much like our mother with her caramel-colored complexion and curly black hair that everybody in the family calls her my mother's "mini-me," after the miniature character in that Austin Powers movie.

She sounds just like my mother too when she adds in that way that is all her own, like an old soul that has been on this earth before, "Dad said he has to work late, they have him working down in Newport today. They work him too hard. I hope he's getting paid over-time."

"Ok. Thank you, honey. I hope so too!" my mother responds and kisses Gabey's cheek and smiling at him before sitting down at the table. "Easter is right around the corner and we have to help Felicia pay for Easter clothes for J.B. and Casey this year. Where's your brother?"

Jaz shrugs her shoulders and widens her eyes to indicate that she has no idea.

"He has a track meet," Aunt Pam says and wipes her hands on a dish towel before joining my mother at the table.

I lean over to give Aunt Pam a hug, and then to hug Jaz before turning to Gabey. His dark brown eyes sparkle when he recognizes me, and he forgets all about the applesauce. He grins and lifts his arms so that I can take him out of the highchair.

"He ate good today," my Aunt Pam says with a smile as I pick him up and kiss his cheeks excessively. "You need to stop nursing him though. It was hard as hell to get him to sleep today."

My mother laughs hard and loud at that. The need to wean my son has been a running family joke since some of his baby teeth had come in, and no matter how many times I try to explain that in Islam babies are usually nursed for two years, they have boatloads of jokes. I smile and roll my eyes with what I hope is my normal, easy- going way, and make my escape.

"I'm heading downstairs to change and to make prayer, I'll be back up in a little bit," I say as I walk towards the stairwell at the opposite side of the kitchen.

"Ok, honey," my mother says, pausing mid-sentence in her conversation with my aunt.

"Ok, Jo, see you later," Aunt Pam says before returning her attention to my mother.

Jaz looks up momentarily from her cell phone to give me a peace sign with her fingers and a grin before going back to her cell phone, most likely texting one of her friends.

Being around my family and holding Gabey in my arms cools much of the anger I had been feeling in the car, but it doesn't get rid of it. I kick off my shoes once I reach the bottom of the stairs and check my watch again. Seven more minutes before I call him.

Asr prayer had already come in so I put Gabriel down into his playpen and turn on the tv, tuning it to PBS kids so I can change out of my work clothes and make wudu. Michael will get some extra time to settle in while I make salaat, and then I will call to say my peace.

The basement is a bit cramped, but there's enough space for our couch and an old reclining chair, a coffee table, a bookshelf, our computer desk, two standing lamps, and a small musalla for making our daily prayers. We have our own bathroom, our own kitchenette, complete with a stove, a refrigerator, and a square table with four chairs; and we were able to split the opposite half of the basement into a bedroom for us and a corner nursery for Gabey.

As I change into a colorful Mumu that I use primarily for prayer, I think about the difficulties of the past year and a half. It has been hard getting used to caring for a baby, and managing a budget, but I had thought that things were finally looking brighter before this announcement had come. Michael had entered his final semester and was only weeks away from getting his degree. The baby was healthy and happy, I'd found a stable job where I can continue my college education once Michael graduates, and there is no rush for us to move out of my parents' house, so we have ample opportunity to save up and to plan for getting a home of our own. No matter how hard I try I can't understand what motivated Michael to marry another wife, so doubt begins to creep into my heart.

Is it me? Is he tired of being married to me? Has he come to think that I'm not compatible with him anymore? Or that I'm not as enthusiastic about Islam as he is?

I take a deep breath and walk over to bathroom to make wudu. The warm water and silent duas soothe my anxious mind and spirit. I try my best to concentrate on preparing for prayer, and on pushing my thoughts aside to quiet my mind. Once done, I walk over to the wide oriental prayer rug near the glass sliding doors that open onto the backyard. I can feel the warm rays of the sun through the glass.

Directly in front of me, an open Quran on a wooden stand sits on top of the low bookshelf beside a wooden incense holder and a glass vase filled with incense sticks. I light an incense stick of sandalwood and amber before draping my scarf over my head and shoulders. Then, facing the east and the late afternoon glow of the sun, I close my eyes and surrender my heart to prayer, and to hope.

Chapter Four

What?!

"You need to calm down, and you need to pray about this," Michael says in his best I know you didn't mean what you-just-said voice. "No one is to blame in this. I love you. This is the will of Allah, and if you will just calm down long enough to pray then you'll realize this."

Thankfully, Gabriel has fallen asleep in his playpen and didn't hear my outburst. I make a mental note to lower my voice, so I don't wake him up. In my defense, I was calm when I had first called him. I didn't have an attitude, and I had even gained enough strength from prayer to be curious about who my new co-wife is, so I had started the conversation pleasantly and with sincere interest, but his revelation is such a blow to the gut that all of my good will flew right out the window.

How could he? How could she? And what?!!! You're where??!!! My head is spinning with feelings of rage, betrayal, and deep heartbreak. He had not only said that his new wife was one of our good friends from college, one of my best friends, Nicole, but that he was at her university campus apartment and did I want to speak to her?! She too lives in Boston is a junior at the same college. I had just answered his question for him with much more visceral candor than he had expected.

I take a deep breath to keep myself from sliding into an abyss of hysteria and I remind myself of the hadeeth that I had recently learned that says something to the effect that if you do not have anything good to say, then you should keep quiet. I purse my lips and allow the heat of angry tears to burn their way down my face. He too keeps quiet on the other side of the telephone. We sit in silence for more than ten minutes before he finally speaks again.

"We probably shouldn't talk about this over the phone. I'll be home tomorrow after jumuah prayer. We can talk about this then," he says tentatively, and I know he is trying to gauge my response.

"Fine," I respond curtly as I angrily swipe at my tears.

"Please don't be like that," he says, and I can hear the pain in his voice, but I can't bring myself to soften up.

"I have to go. As Salaamu Alaikum," I say, just barely keeping my voice from breaking as the tears continue to fall.

He takes a deep breath and replies, "Walaikum as salaam."

I hang up before he can say anything else, and I bury my face into the pillow so I can cry without waking up the baby. I'd thought that I was done crying, but my heart said, nope, you've got to go through this, girl.

I cry over what I imagine he is saying to Nicole right now. I cry over all the times during the past four months when I'd tried to call him and he hadn't picked up the phone, and I now imagine that it had been because he had been with Nicole. I cry over imagined slights and dreamed-up situations of disrespect, all the while wishing that he would come back home and look me in the eyes to explain how he could have done this.

I finally cry myself to sleep and I don't wake up until I hear Galwy crying from where he is now standing up in the playpen. I look around in the darkness for the bedside table and turn on the lamp. The sun has set, and my watch reveals that it is 7:30pm. We'd slept for over two hours. I walk over to the playpen and pick him up, holding him close to me.

"I'm sorry, baby. Mommy fell asleep," I croon as I kiss his little face.

He stops crying and lays his head on my shoulder, wrapping his arms around my neck. My eyes feel puffy and gritty from all the crying I've done, and I can just imagine what they must look like. I can hear my father's loud, boisterous laughter from the kitchen upstairs, and I know instinctively that he and probably everyone else in the family is sitting around the table or standing around the kitchen talking. I can smell that someone has cooked, most likely Aunt Pam, and my stomach rumbles hungrily, but I don't want to risk going upstairs and having to explain my puffy eyes.

Gabey starts falling back to sleep in my arms so I venture over to the kitchenette to see what I have in the refrigerator. Deciding that I don't want cold cereal or a turkey and cheese sandwich, I settle on a Nutri Grain bar and a bottle of water. I go back to the bed and I lean back against the headboard, laying Gabriel beside me so that he can nestle against my waist. He settles back into a peaceful sleep within seconds. Once I'm sure that he is really sleeping I open the Nutri Grain bar and reach for the remote control to change the channel and to try to distract myself from my pitiful, heartbroken thoughts.

I channel surf for a few seconds, then I hear the sound of a car driving up to the front of the house. Our bed is pushed against the north wall of the house that faces the street so we can hear whenever a car is coming or going; I hear the car door open and close, and then I hear Michael's deep voice thank someone for the ride.

My heart skips a beat, and then softens as I hear his footsteps coming up the driveway. He had to have gotten off the phone with me and gone straight to the train station to have made it to Rhode Island so quickly. I swallow the bite of the Nutri Grain bar and wash it down with a gulp from the bottle of water before gently easing myself off the bed and tiptoeing across the basement to the stairs. I hear his key in the lock and step back into the shadows, so he won't see me if he looks down the stairs. Someone in the kitchen has also heard the car and the footsteps along the driveway – it's my dad. He meets Michael at the door and welcomes him boisterously.

"Hey! What are you doing here? Done with school and work already for the week?" I hear my father say.

I hear Michael respond, "Yeah, I took a much-needed day off for tomorrow. Luckily I have some vacation days and was able to talk to my professors."

Their footsteps drift off into the kitchen and I can vaguely hear Michael greet the rest of the family. I take the opportunity to rush over to the bathroom to wash my tear-stained face. I splash cold water on it and peer at myself in the mirror. My eyelids are puffy and sore to the touch from so much crying, and my hair is tangled and matted on one side. I dry my face, noticing a slight sallowness under my dark brown complexion from lack of sleep this past week, and I run a brush through my flat-ironed hair. I take a deep breath. I want to be angry, and I want to be firm with indignation, but I'm happy, and I feel weak.

I'm standing in front of the sink in the bathroom when I hear Michael coming down the stairs. I turn around and take a step forward into the open bathroom doorway to face him. He still has his jacket on, and he's carrying his backpack on his shoulder while holding his duffle bag in his hand. I stand frozen in the doorway, wanting to go to him, but suddenly unsure of what his presence here means.

Had he rushed here because he's angry and he wants to have it out with me? I'd been ignoring his calls all week, and then I'd gone and basically hung up on him when I finally did call. He doesn't look angry, however, as he takes off his jacket and drops it and his bags onto the couch to the right of the stairs. He's wearing a green hoodie that contrasts nicely against the honey-brown of his complexion, and jeans, and his light brown eyes are warm and tentative as he takes a few steps forward. He stops halfway across the room, next to where our little breakfast table and chairs are set up.

"As Salaamu Alaikum," he says quietly, glancing over at the bed where Gabriel is still fast asleep.

I self-consciously smooth my hair back from my face and adjust the collar of the bright pink Mumu I'm wearing, embarrassed that my eyes give me away no matter how much I want to appear unbothered.

"Wasalaamu Alaikum," I say, and I also take a few steps towards him, not quite reaching the table, but close enough to speak freely without waking Gabey.

Michael looks uncomfortable when I don't say anything else, and we stand there, watching each other for several seconds before he finally asks, "Can we talk now?"

His eyes plead with mine as he grips the back of one of the chairs. I nod and walk over to chair opposite him and sit down. He heaves a sigh of relief and pulls out the chair he's been holding onto to sit down too.

Once we both sit, he places his hands on the table and says, "I apologize for the way I handled this. Please forgive me, Jo. We can take this slowly so you can get used to this whole thing. Please don't be angry. We can work through this."

It's hard for me to imagine how, but I don't shut him down and I instead lower my gaze to my folded hands in my lap. Nicole is a friend, a close friend, and that means that she's known about this; that she had gone through with the marriage ceremony without saying a word to me about it.

Just the thought makes hot, angry tears well up in my throat, but I swallow hard against them and summon every ounce of reason that I can, so I don't fall into the abyss of the wild and instinctive urge I have to lash out. I close my eyes and take a deep breath and say nothing. He speaks again.

"She wants to talk to you. She doesn't want you to be upset either. Have you prayed about this yet? If you can take some time to pray about this, I know you'll feel better and you'll understand," he says gently.

I open my eyes and look at him. His expression is sincere and earnest. I stare at him, seeing him for the first time in a new light. He hadn't made this decision lightly, and I can tell that he is rooted in a faith-based space. In Islam it's called Taqwa: when we function primarily, and to the best of our ability, from a place where we are mindful of God in our decision making and actions. I can also sense that he is expecting me to function from that same space.

I admit to myself that he has spoken about polygyny and his interest in having more than one wife numerous times, but I had never taken him seriously. I just hadn't been in a head space where I had considered what he had been saying with consciousness of God in mind. I'd thought that he was joking, that it was just talk to stir up the conversation whenever women were around.

As I think back to some of those conversations now all I remember is how easily he had been able to get a rise out of my friends or cousins, and how combative women on campus or at the university student union would get when he mentioned it. I'd honestly never considered him actually going through with the process for real, especially without discussing the details of it with me first.

Feeling exhausted and emotionally drained I finally say, "No, I haven't prayed about it."

"Why not?" he asks, surprised and sincerely curious.

"Because I've been too upset about it," I answer defensively.

Frustrated, and torn between humbling myself to the principals of a believer and giving into the rage of my emotions, I sigh deeply and lean forward at the table to hold my head in my hands. This is not what I expected to have to go through when I'd embraced Islam. On the one hand I feel like I've been ambushed and on the other I feel like I'm falling short of the goal.

When I consider polygyny in the light of God consciousness, with Taqwa, I can't help but admit that I'm being selfish and obstinate in my reactions. The Quran is clear about permitting a husband to marry up to four women, and if I really believe in the Quran, and not just in the parts of the Quran that I like, then how can I not turn to

God in prayer about this? Another silence develops between us, this one more tense and longer than the last one.

"Will you?" he finally asks. "Will you pray about it?"

We stare at each other again. Countless thoughts run through my head. I center myself around the foundation of our relationship and how it has been built upon prayer. We had been passionate and a little naïve early on in our relationship, but despite that, we had prayerfully entered into our marriage. We had prayerfully taken on the responsibility of having our son, and we had prayerfully converted to Islam from Christianity. How can I now decide to ignore the principal of prayer when faced with this, no matter how painful?

"Yes, I'll pray about it," I finally answer.

He smiles widely and sighs with relief, dropping his head into his hands as if he'd really thought that I might have said no.

"Thank you," he says earnestly, his voice thick with emotion, and he reaches his hand across the table for mine.

I don't know if it's subconscious on his part, but he always does this when he knows that I'm reluctant about a request that he's making to me. Whether it's him asking me to get out of bed to make him a cup of coffee when I'm really comfortable or asking me to change Gabey even when it's his turn but Gabriel has left a little something in his diaper that he doesn't want to clean. He'll reach out his hand to me, or with a smile or a playful grin.

In this moment, I can't smile, my heart is too heavy, but I reach over and give him my hand. That, at least, is a start.

Chapter Five

Istikharah

The next morning, I call out of work, letting my supervisor Carol know that I will be taking a personal day.

"Ok, that's fine. It's quiet here today anyway. I hope you're feeling ok," she says.

I smile half-heartedly, grateful for her concern and for having her as a co-worker. Carol is one of the coolest white women I know, and not because she works with me at the Center for the Study of Race and Ethnicity in America, but because her energy is so mellow. We interact with high energy (sometimes wild and obnoxious) college students daily and she never loses her cool, or her empathy.

I had come into work on Monday so upset that I had slammed my work bag onto my desk, which had echoed through the almost empty first floor of the building. She soon came into my office to check on me, and when I saw her calm demeanor and caring expression, I almost broke down in tears.

She had asked me if I was ok, and I had made up an excuse that I can't remember at the moment, then she had given me a hug and had said that if I needed anything, she was right across the hall. I hadn't been myself for the remainder of the week and although she'd noticed, she hadn't pried or made any demands of me.

"Yeah, I'm ok, Thanks Carol. It's been a tough week but I'm feeling better today. Hopefully by Monday everything will be sorted out," I say.

As co-workers go, I consider her a friend and we talk about personal stuff often, but I hadn't had the emotional strength to mention anything to her. I would eventually, of that, I am sure.

"Ok," she says, in her lilting, laid-back way, her tone letting me know that she would wait until I was ready to talk about it. "Take care of yourself and tell that husband of yours that he'd better be treating you right."

I laugh politely but it isn't in my heart, and I reply, "I will. Have a nice weekend."

"You too," she responds.

I hang up and stare at the telephone receiver in a daze. Michael and Gabriel are still asleep downstairs, and dad had just left for work, taking James and Jasmine with him to drop them off at school on the way. Aunt Pam is in the kitchen making a pot of coffee and my mother is still upstairs in her bedroom getting dressed for work.

Mom and I usually drive into work together, but she would know right away when she saw me that I wouldn't be going in today. I sit in the living on the love seat for a while, first staring at the telephone receiver and then out the window.

Last night had been terrible. Michael and I had eaten a dinner of turkey sandwiches and potato chips at our little table in the basement and although he had tried to make light conversation with me, I couldn't muster the energy or the patience to respond with more than one-word answers, or by shrugging my shoulders. Thankfully Gabriel woke up which gave me an excuse to go upstairs because I'd left his highchair up there.

I'd taken my time warming up the baby food and feeding him, then I'd taken him to the second-floor bathroom to bathe him and had let him play in the shallow, bubble-filled water until his fingers and toes were wrinkly. When I'd finally made it back downstairs Michael was fast asleep, still fully clothed, and all 6 feet 3 inches of him sprawled tiredly across the queen-sized bed. I'd rocked Gabey to sleep in the rocking chair and then placed him into his crib to sleep for the night before laying myself down on the couch.

Feeling exhausted and drained of all motivation to do anything at all, I had just laid on the couch all night, thinking, crying, tossing and turning. When Fajr prayer had come in, I mustered the energy to get up to make wudu then I prayed my fard salaat and offered two rakaats of salaatul istikharah afterwards. Once I'd finished, I sat on the prayer rug, trying not to cry and making dua to Allah for guidance.

Although it hadn't taken all of the pain away, the prayer had given me peace, and after watching the basement brighten with the rising of the sun, I'd finally walked upstairs to sit quietly in the living room before making the call to my job.

"Hey! Why aren't you dressed?" my mother asks as she comes down the stairs and sees me sitting on the love seat in the same pink Mumu, I'd been wearing the night before.

"I just called out," I tell her as she reaches me and leans over to give me a hug.

She frowns when she notices my puffy eyes and asks, "I take it that it didn't go well last night?"

I shake my head no and she pats my cheek. Aunt Pam walks into the living room and stands next to my mother.

"Why are you two whispering? What's going on?" she demands, frustrated. "Nobody tells me nothing around here! What's wrong, Jo? Why have you been crying so much?"

My mother kisses my cheek and hugs her sister before saying, "I have to go. Jo, call me later."

Aunt Pam's jaw drops open to object as my mother turns and hurries out of the room, but my mother is too fast and is gone before Aunt Pam can say anything. She turns to me and grabs my hand, pulling me up off the love seat to drag me into the kitchen.

"Come on," she says as we walk, me dragging my feet. "I'm going to make you a cup of coffee and you're going to tell me what's going on."

She makes me sit down at the kitchen table and crosses over to the counter to make me a cup of coffee. She adds creamer and sugar to it, brings the mug over to me, and sits down next to me, pulling her chair close.

"Spill it," she says in a no-nonsense tone.

My maternal grandmother had passed away when I was little, and Aunt Pam is the eldest in the family on that side. Her and my mother look a lot alike, but she's taller, and her skin tone is fairer. She and my mother are very close, and she's been a fixture in our family for as long as I can remember. She'd never had any children of her own. Very much the matriarch, she'd moved in with us when she had retired from her job at one of the large banks downtown, and now she stays in the spare bedroom to help out financially.

The only reason I hadn't told her yet is because of the news I'd gotten yesterday. She loves Nicole, just like everyone else in the family, and I still don't want to tell any of them about this. I decide to tread carefully with what I will reveal, at least until I'm completely sure about whether I'm going to sign onto this or not.

I take a deep breath and begin.

"Well. You know that Michal and I have converted to Islam, and well, in Islam, a man can marry up to four wives according to Islamic law and," I say but I don't get to finish my sentence.

She's gotten the gist and has put enough together about my behavior for the past week to have a pretty good idea of what I'm going to say.

"Oh no! I don't think so! Have you told your father? Where is Michael? He's downstairs, isn't he," she exclaims and springs up from her chair, whirling in the direction of the basement; I also jump up and hold onto her arm to stop her.

"Auntie, please," I beg, pulling her back to the chair and forcing her to sit back down. "The baby is still sleeping, and I don't want you to make a big deal out of this. Let me finish."

She is furious: breathing heavy and fast through her nose, her forehead is all creased-up from frowning, and her cheeks are flushed. If this is her reaction to just the concept of polygyny, then I'm definitely not about to tell her any specifics. She gradually begins to calm down as I keep my hand on her arm, trying to pin her to the chair with my sheer willpower. I continue as calmly as possible.

"So. As you've guessed, Michael has decided that he wants to marry a second wife," I say, keeping eye contact the entire time and being as honest as I can be about my feelings. "I'm struggling with it, but like you and mom, I'm a praying woman too, and I just started praying about this. And I'll be honest, I was too hurt and angry to pray about it before now, but I prayed about it this morning and I'm finally at peace with it. Now I just have to decide if this is something that I want to do with my life."

"You two haven't even been married for three years! How can he possibly know that he wants another wife when the two of you have just started with your own marriage?!" she demands rhetorically. "I thought he was studying to be a preacher, or an Imam or whatever? This doesn't sound very holy to me."

I don't know what to say to that because the wound from finding out about this is way too raw, and I'm still harboring some of the same kind of resentment.

Metaphorically speaking, the bleeding has stopped, thanks be to God, but now I have to heal. He'd made the effort to come home last night, in spite of the responsibilities that he has in Boston today at school and work, and that at least shows me that our relationship is a priority.

"He has the right to his own choices, Auntie," is the best that I can come up with in response.

She snorts derisively but doesn't say anything.

"You've told me plenty of times yourself, Auntie: life is filled with hard truths. This is one of them," I say in response to her snort, remembering the talks we had during high school and how she used those same words on me.

It's amazing that those words have stuck with me. I didn't always want to hear what she had to say back then, but more often than not, she had been right. And this really is a hard truth. I can't force him to stop with this effort for plural marriage any more than he can force me to join with him in it.

Upon thinking about it, I honestly don't want to be that woman who makes demands and tries to stifle or restrict her husband's motivations. If this is what he believes is God's will for his life, who am I to tell him otherwise? All I can do is decide if this is also what God wills for me.

Aunt Pam's light brown eyes fill with tears and she covers my hand with hers as she says, "Look at you. My sweet girl all grown up. I hear you, but there are some things in this world that you don't have to pray about. There are some things that you can just reject for what they are: wrong!"

I lower my head and sigh deeply. She is speaking the emotions that I have been wrestling with all week long. I don't think polygyny is wrong, how could it be if God permits it? But right now, in this moment, it feels wrong. Something deep within me wants to scream at the top of my lungs about how wrong it feels and about how painful it is, but the thought that came to me last night as I had tossed and turned was: if it is wrong would God have said that it is ok for men, and women, to enter into such relationships?

"I know that, Auntie, but how can I say that this is wrong if the scriptures that I believe in say that it's permitted by God? And there are even stories in the bible where believers have more than one wife?" I reply, hoping she'll answer me.

I can't deny that some of the most inspirational women of Judaism, Christianity and Islam had entered into such polygynous or polygamous relationships, especially when I'm personally faced with such an important decision.

Before going away to college, I had begun seeking a closer relationship with God, and when Michael and I met, he was like the manifestation of an answered prayer. We have only just begun walking together in faith, and I don't want to reject something that God may want for me.

She meets my gaze head on, but it takes her a few thoughtful moments to respond.

"That's a really good question, honey," she finally replies and continues hesitantly. "And it's not an easy question to answer. I can only answer for myself, and all I can say is that what might be right for one person may not be right for another. I can't say that polygamy is wrong, but I *can* say that I've seen enough in this life to know that situations where there's one man vying for the affections of more than one woman have ended badly, if they end at all. Some of them just keep going, and going, and spiraling downward into deeper and deeper levels of chaos."

I listen intently, grateful for her words and aware that my decision will not only affect me. This decision will affect my little boy and his relationship with his father, it will affect the nature of the life and family that I've envisioned for myself, and it will affect my extended family and the relationships that we all have with one another too. I have to ask myself questions like: do I want to be a divorced, single mother? Do I really want to give up on a marriage and a relationship that is so fledgling that it hadn't even matured enough to spread its wings? Do I want to risk the tension and hostility that may arise from family members and friends that disagree with my choice?

Aunt Pam wipes the tears from her eyes and watches me carefully, reading the emotions displayed upon my face as I battle with these thoughts.

She finally says with a voice full of love and compassion, "I see that you're sincerely considering this, honey. I can't tell you what to do, but I can tell you that I don't want this kind of struggle for you. Plural marriage, polygamy, polygyny, whatever . . . it might not be wrong, but I can tell you, it will not be easy. Believe me, I know what it's like. I may not have been married to your uncle Frank, God rest his soul, but I had to deal with his ex-wives and baby-mommas, and that was a hardship I wouldn't wish on anybody. Women can be mean, petty, and all kinds of jealous, and situations involving jealousy over men can bring out the worst in you. You have to be aware of that, honey, not only for others, but for yourself too . . .You go ahead and continue to pray on it. And I'll support you no matter what you decide."

Tears of relief fill my eyes and I realize how much her support means to me. This whole situation is daunting, and I don't want to face it alone. As if reading my mind, she opens her arms for a hug and I quickly lean right in. She holds me for several long, warm minutes – for so long that I smell like her cocoa butter lotion when she lets me go – and then she kisses my cheek and pulls away to look at me. We smile tentatively at each other, her with the wisdom of knowing what I might have to face, and me with the hope that I will make the right decision.

She finally shakes her head and laughs, lightening the mood and picking up her coffee cup to say, "God bless you if you have to tell your father about this, honey. Michael better not be around when you do."

Chapter Six

Coming to Terms

Aunt Pam had insisted that I go relax and take a long, hot shower after we'd talked, and she had promised that she would get the baby if she heard him wake up. When she saw my hesitation, she had in addition promised that she'd be nice to Michael. I stipulated that she couldn't roll her eyes at him, or huff and puff under her breath murmuring rude comments around him, and that she had to treat him in the same loving way that she had up until now. She'd rolled her eyes up to the ceiling in exasperation, but she'd agreed.

Feeling a little stiff from tossing and turning on the couch all night, but more at peace than earlier, I walk quietly down the stairs to the basement to do as she says. Gabriel and Michael are still fast asleep, but Gabey must have woken up at some point because he is now on our bed beside Michael, spooned against Michael's chest with his mouth slightly open and sleeping as deeply as his father. I get some clean clothes from the dresser and tiptoe into the bathroom to shower.

The strong stream of hot water is just what I need. I stay under it for as long as I can, taking my time washing my hair and allowing the water to massage the tension from my back and shoulders. Once clean, and relaxed, I decide that I'm going to give polygyny with Nicole a try. I've weighed all of the pros and cons as much as I can, and I decide that the pros win.

Pro #1: God has permitted it in the scriptures and in the Quran, so it has to have benefit to it.

Pro #2: I will honor my marriage vows and keep our little family intact.

Pro #3: We love each other, and as long as we keep God first in our lives and in our marriage then I'm willing to see what polygyny can add to us.

Pro #4: Nicole is my friend, and despite the circumstances, I love her.

Now I just need to hear from him that he wants to stay married to me, and that this isn't his way of trying to somehow get out of our marriage. In my heart I don't think it is, but I need to hear it from him . . . When the water begins to get cool, I force myself to get out of the shower, to towel dry my hair, and to take my time to moisturize, smoothing lotion on leisurely and paying special attention to my feet – they had been neglected all winter and I definitely needed to invest in a loofa. And soon.

I get dressed in the bathroom, not wanting to take a chance waking Michael or Gabey, but I start sweating so I open the bathroom door to let out some of the steam. I peek around the open door to check on Gabriel and to my surprise the bed is empty. I dump my dirty clothes into the laundry basket and cautiously go back upstairs. I can hear Aunt

Pam and Michael talking as I reach the threshold of the kitchen.

"You're pretty good at this, as far as fathers go," Aunt Pam says as I enter the kitchen and smiles covertly at me with self-satisfaction before complimenting Michael again. "You don't make too much of a mess, and you don't put too much on the spoon either."

He laughs comfortably as she places a cup of coffee beside his elbow, and he spoons a mix of cereal and applesauce into Gabriel's mouth.

"You look refreshed," Aunt Pam says to me as I reach the table.

"I feel refreshed," I reply and sit down in the chair beside Gabriel's highchair.

"Mama, mama, mama," Gabriel says happily when he sees me, splattering applesauce and oatmeal all over his face.

Michael and I look at each other briefly, both of us trying to get an idea of how the other is feeling, before looking back at Aunt Pam.

"I was just keeping your husband company until you came upstairs. I have some errands to run this morning, and then I have my book club, so I'll say good day to you three," she says and kisses my cheek, giving my shoulder a squeeze of encouragement.

Michael stands up to hug her and she smiles bashfully as she hugs him back. She kisses Gabey's forehead and leaves the kitchen to go upstairs. Michael sits back down and gives Gabriel another spoonful of breakfast.

"Good morning. You look nice. I love you in yellow," Michael says, and I know he's searching for neutral ground for conversation.

"Good morning. Thanks," I reply and search through my mind for a verbal olive branch to extend to him. "I was hoping that we might be able to make it to jumuah today, to pray in the masjid."

His eyes brighten and he eagerly agrees to the suggestion.

"Yes. That sounds perfect. Gabey's big enough to stay with me in the men's section if you want. He should be fine as long as he can't see you," Michael says with a smile and in an attempt for light-heartedness.

I return the smile as best as I can. It hurts a little, but I manage. I want this to work out. We'd taken vows to each other. Granted, he'd also taken vows to another, but regardless of that fact, there is still us, and if he truly wants to stay married to me, then I want to give this a try.

"I need to ask you something, first, though," I say, and my heart picks up its pace.

He gives me his full attention and nods solemnly as he spoons more applesauce for Gabey.

"I know that this year hasn't been great. Do you want to stay married to me?" I find the courage to ask.

He looks shocked and hurt that I would even ask him that and replies, "Of course I do. Why would you say that?"

"Well, it seems obvious to me. You got married to another woman in secret without telling me," I say, then I hope I've conveyed that without too much heat.

"Not because I don't want to be married to you," he replies defensively.

"Then why?" I ask.

He's quiet for a few seconds before answering, "I don't know. I guess because deep down I knew that I might lose you if I told you. I still feel like I might."

I nod thoughtfully but don't say anything else. He's finished feeding Gabriel his breakfast, so he hands him his sippy cup of juice.

"Am I going to lose you?" he finally asks, his voice low.

I shrug my shoulders and respond, "I don't know. I don't want you to. I don't want to lose you either."

No tears form in my throat or prick at my eyes this time, though. This time when I think about the possibilities for us, I feel calm. If I chose to stay, it might hurt for a while; and if I leave it might hurt for a while, but either way, I know that I will go on living. It's just a matter of coming to terms with whether I will go on living with him as my husband or without him.

"I'll take over with Gabey if you want to go and take a shower," I offer into the silence.

"Ok. Yeah," he says and stands up.

Gabey puts down his sippy cup and smiles at me, clapping his hands happily as I sit down in the chair Michael had been sitting in, and I smile back, mainly because of all of the cereal and applesauce that's all over his cheeks and chin. I wipe off the excess with the receiving blanket draped over the back of his highchair and remove the tray from in front of him.

Michael goes downstairs and I pick Gabriel up and carry him upstairs for a bath. While he plays and splashes in the bubbles, I sit on the closed toilet seat and watch him, imagining what it will be like for him to grow up in a polygynous family. He's already attached to Nicole. After all, I'd chosen her and my best friend Lisa to be his Godmothers. And I know that she loves him too. She is already like a second mom to him when she comes to visit.

I also think about my family and how my parents consider her as their "other daughter;" and how my brother and sister think of her as another sister. She and I had met during our freshman year of college too, before we'd met Michael and his friends, and because she had travelled up north for school and couldn't always get back down south during the holidays, she had become a fixture in our house on Thanksgiving and on weekends when I had come back home.

My gut wrenches as I consider her relationship with Michael. Why hadn't I noticed anything? There hadn't been any warning signs or obvious signals. I hadn't ever imagined that the two of them had anything other than friendly feelings for each other. She'd actually spent Thanksgiving with us last year and thinking back, I couldn't remember anything that indicated that they were more than just friends.

"I'm ready when you are," Michael says, smiling as he enters the bathroom, and interrupting my thoughts. "I figure, since it's so early, we can drive out to the big masjid in North Smithfield – we can make a day of it – stop for coffee and a little something to eat before jumuah."

I smile back and stand up to reach for Gabey's wash cloth before replying, "Ok. That sounds nice. I'll wash him up now and bring him downstairs to get him dressed."

"Ok. Good. I'll go and get a little reading done while I wait," he says and turns to go back downstairs.

I wash Gabey, rinsing the suds off thoroughly, then I wrap him up in a soft towel and pull the plug from the drain in the bathtub, leaving the baby toys to float around in the water as it empties. I carry Gabey downstairs, despite his wriggling to get down. He's desperate to climb down the stairs by himself.

"Down! Get down!" he says vehemently as he squirms in my arms, getting me wet in the process and forcing me to squeeze him tightly to my chest which only increases the wetness.

"No," I say firmly, willing him to stop. "Want to go to the masjid? We're going to the masjid today. Let's go get dressed."

He pauses and looks curiously up at me, as if his 18-month-old brain is trying to remember what the masjid is.

"Math-pid?" he says.

I laugh at his cute little lisp and reply, "Yes! Masjid. To make prayer."

"Make pway-er," he repeats happily, letting me know that he knows at least that part of what I'm talking about by lifting his small, chubby arms up with his hands beside each of his ears, mimicking one of the movements of salaat.

"Yes, prayer," I say, smiling and pleased in a way that only a mother can be when she sees that her child has internalized some of the things that she's taught him.

I hold him close to me, smiling and more determined to be sure that I'm making the right decision. We reach the basement and Michael smiles up at us from his seat on the couch where he's reading with is notebooks opened around him and a pen in his hand.

Much of the tension is now gone from between us and I can feel us settling back into the rhythm that our little family has developed. I lay Gabey on the bed to put lotion on him and then I cover his little bottom with a pamper. I let him go to crawl around on the bed while I select his clothes and he scurries away from me as soon as I let him go, making quick work of maneuvering his squat little body off the bed. Then, with a wild, victorious laugh, he goes straight for the stairs as soon as his feet touch the floor.

Michael reaches a long arm out from his seat on the couch and scoops him up before he can reach the first step, and he squeals loudly with laughter at the shock of having been stopped before reaching his goal.

"Where do you think you're going?" Michael says as he stands up and tosses Gabey up into the air, then catches him.

Gabriel is hysterical with laughter at this point, familiar with this exchange. Michael tosses him up and catches him two more times before walking him over to me, cradling him in his arms, and laughing right along with him. I smile uncontrollably and happily, and in that moment, I know that everything is going to be ok.

Our little family is young, but it is strong, and there is plenty of room for adding another person to love; someone that we actually already love.

Chapter Seven

Woman to Woman

Two weeks later, when the day finally arrives for Nicole and me to see each other face to face, I'm an emotional wreck. It's the third week of May so the weather is warm, almost hot, and the sun is bright against a cloudless sky. It's a picturesque and almost perfect Saturday. Someone rides past the train station on a bike; and a couple plays frisbee on the lawn near the Capitol building across the street . . . but I feel slightly dizzy, and my stomach is so full of butterflies that I can hardly breathe.

She and I had agreed to go to a coffee shop close by the station where we could sit at an outside table and talk, but I'm ready to back out of it. We'd talked on the phone for about fifteen minutes a week ago and it was one of the weirdest, most uncomfortable conversations that I had ever had. It had been hard for me to concentrate on what she was saying because I was terrified that she would say too much about something that she and Michael had done together; and on top of that, Michael had been sitting on the couch across the room from me, pretending to be working but I could feel him listening to my every word. Hopefully today would be much easier.

Michael had stayed home with the baby and I had taken the bus to meet her at the train station. She is taking the T into

Providence from Boston and the coffee shop is within walking distance. We haven't seen each other since early December so this is going to be our first encounter as co-wives . . . I adjust my light blue headscarf self-consciously as I wait for her outside of the station.

The last time that she and I had spoken before last Saturday was almost five months ago, sometime in January, and, come to find out, it was around the time when she and Michael had gotten married. I couldn't for the life of me remember the full conversation that we'd had, but I was pretty sure that she hadn't said anything about marriage, or a boyfriend, or being interested in anyone: nothing at all about her love life, and that hurt more than I wanted to admit.

I'd prayed about it last night and I had tried to make peace with it by rationalizing that she may not have known what to say, but it was hard to push the feelings of betrayal away. This meeting will be the test to see if she and I can interact with each other while keeping our friendship intact.

I peer across the sidewalk towards the front entrance of the train station and see her approaching. My stomach lurches nervously at the sight of her. Tall and slender with a smooth coffee colored complexion and a bright, charismatic smile, she has a natural friendly way about her that usually puts me right at ease, but not today. Today, as I watch her gracefully walk towards me with that bright, kind smile, I want to turn and hurry off in the opposite direction.

We usually hug when we see each other and I wonder if she is going to try to hug me, or if I should hug her if she doesn't. She reaches me and pauses momentarily, as if having the same doubts I'm having, then opens her arms for a hug. We hug awkwardly and briefly.

"As Salaamu Alaikum," she says, still smiling. "You look pretty! I got you something! How are you?"

My heart tightens in my chest as she hands me a pretty gift bag, but I manage to smile back and reply, "Wasalaamu Alaikum. Thank you. You do too. I'm fine. How are you?"

"I'm good! Al hamdulilah! Glad to be off the train. It's so nice out today!" she says in her usual joyful and enthusiastic way.

I don't feel even close to as joyful or enthusiastic so I smile as best as I can and start walking towards the coffee shop. She falls in step beside me with ease and continues to make conversation.

"I'm so happy to be here. This is going to be great; don't you think?" she says and peers over at me with a smile, as if we are about to go on a great adventure together.

Caught off guard I reply, "I, uh, well, I hope so. It will be nice to talk and to see if we're on the same page."

She nods in agreement and responds, "Yes, it will, I've been wanting to talk. And I think we are. Islam says that it is permissible, and Allah knows best."

I can't argue with that, no matter how my heart aches. I nod and smile stiffly but it feels more like a grimace. We walk in silence for a few minutes before she speaks again.

"I wanted to call you weeks ago," she says and waits for a response.

I don't know what to say to that. Michael had told me as much, but I hadn't wanted to be the one to call, and he'd never said that she'd intended to. And it was Michael who had facilitated our phone call the previous weekend by handing me the phone before I could get away.

I can't think of anything good or nice to say, so I respond with, "Hmm?"

She repeats, a little more firmly this time, "I wanted to call you weeks ago."

All the hurt feelings of betrayal well up in my chest and I can't stop myself from blurting accusingly, "Why didn't you?"

She seems shocked and saddened by my tone and replies, "I didn't think it was the right time."

We are almost at the coffee shop and I can smell the pleasant aromas in the air, but I suddenly don't want to sit around a lot of strangers and have coffee. I don't want any pretense or religiosity between us: I want to talk – heart to heart – woman to woman – friend to friend.

"Can we go over to the park instead of the coffee shop?" I ask her, gesturing towards Water Place Park not too far a walk away. "Where we can just talk and be honest with each other about everything?"

She nods enthusiastically.

We begin walking again and cross the street, reaching Kennedy Plaza on the left. The Saturday bus schedule is in effect so there aren't as many buses idling or driving through the plaza as there usually are which is nice, and quieter than usual. We walk past people lounging on a bench waiting for their bus; and a group of teenagers run around us, headed for the Providence rink where they have just opened up for roller skating.

We reach the edge of the park and descend the few steps that lead towards a pair of empty benches by the river. This area is well isolated, and no one is sitting within earshot, so I gesture to Nicole, seeing if she wants to sit here.

She nods and we sit down facing each other under the shade of Maple trees with the afternoon sun at our backs.

We sit quietly and expectantly for what feels like the longest seconds of my life before we both start talking at the same time. We both stop talking at the same time too, looking at each other awkwardly and smiling politely at each other before she gestures for me to go.

"It's taken a lot of prayers and soul searching for me to get to this point, and I'm still working out some kinks internally," I admit, meeting her gaze squarely. "It's not a decision that I came to lightly. The main reason that I'm going to give this a try is for the sake of Allah. I prayed istikharah twice, and with each prayer I felt more at peace."

"I've prayed about this too," she agrees earnestly. "I haven't married Michael to hurt you, Joanna. I married him because I believe that it is what Allah has willed for me."

I'm sure that she believes that this is God's will for her, and it comforts me to hear it, but it still hurts a little. I want to ask her what had brought her and Michael to this decision, and why hadn't they at least invited me to the wedding, but I realize that those questions will just lead me down the slippery slope of making judgements about their decisions. Our choices have been made. Now it's time to come to terms with those choices, and to try to move forward together.

"I understand, and I believe you. I haven't told my family or anyone about this yet. Just my mother and Aunt Pam. I wanted to talk to you first," I say, sticking to practical matters and trying to keep my feelings out of it.

She nods and replies, "Yes, Michael told me. Whenever you think it's a good time to tell them is good for me. I haven't told my family yet either."

"Michael told me that too," I respond. "I think we all agree that we should wait until we've gotten things lined up for the summer so that they'll know we're being responsible. The plan is for him to start working full time with Dr. Qadhi at the masjid after he graduates next week, I'll stay on at my job and apply for continuing my degree next spring, and he said that you'll be working at an internship this summer in Boston then starting back in the fall for your senior year?"

"Yes," she answers. "I've already found an off-campus apartment. Hopefully I'll be able to keep it next year too."

It's a relief that we can at least talk about this part of our new relationship freely. I want to bring up how I feel betrayed, but as I look at her earnest, sincere expression, full of an eagerness to compromise and to be kind, I simply can't.

There's a pause in the conversation as both of us search internally for something to say. Thoughts about how we will maneuver through the details of Michael's schedule, about living arrangements, and about travelling and budgeting flit through my head, but we still have time to figure that out. Most importantly, from this meeting, I had wanted to get a sense of if we would be able to talk to each and to be around each other without too much tension or negativity, and so far, so good.

Fortunately, neither of us are combative by nature, and generally speaking, it feels the same way that it had always felt between us. Our friendship has always been easy because we have such similar temperaments and from what I can tell so far, this isn't going to be a tug of war with me holding onto Michael on one side and her holding onto him from the other.

"I figure, as we get used to the dynamics with each other, we can ease into telling our families over the summer," I suggest tentatively into the silence. "I think they'll take it much better if they know we're determined and in one accord, or that we are at least working towards a common goal; and that we aren't angry or upset with one another."

"I agree," Nicole says with a sigh of relief. "It's been hard enough to get Mama to understand why I converted to Islam. It's going to be even harder to get her to accept this."

An image of her mom, Ms. Angeline, the epitome of southern Christian womanhood, hearing that her eldest daughter had entered into a plural marriage flashes across my mind and compassion washes over me. This isn't going to be easy for any of us. I suspect that even Michael's mother is going to object.

"I hear you. I don't know how I'm going to tell my dad," I say thoughtfully. "But as long as we stay focused on treating one another with respect and with kindness, and on building a family that is loving and secure, I don't think he or anyone will be able to object too much."

She nods and says, "I agree. We have to do this right. For the sake of Allah first and above everything else."

I nod and we sit in silence again, before Nicole speaks.

"I just want to say, I love you. I want this to work, and part of why I even said yes to Michael is because I love you so much. I don't want this to change our friendship," she says, and I can see the wetness forming in her eyes.

The saying goes, "God works in mysterious ways," and in this moment, all of the angst and discomfort that I've been feeling disappears. A feeling of love, of calm and of peace envelopes me, compelling me to reach out and to give her a hug.

"I love you too," I say, and I hope that she can feel that love from my hug.

We hug for at least a minute before letting go of each other and when she smiles at me this time, I'm able to genuinely smile back, hopeful that this won't be as hard as I expect it to be.

"You wanna go and get some coffee now?" she asks.

"Yes, please!" I respond, so relieved to have gotten through this meeting without losing myself or our friendship that a trip to the coffee shop sounds like the perfect reward. "They have these new cranberry and orange scones that are so good! You're going to love them."

And like that, we fall into a rhythm that's familiar in many ways, but careful and tentative in others. Only time will tell where we go from here.

Chapter Eight

Girlfriends

"Wait. Wait. Wait a minute," Lisa says, every trace of humor gone from her face and tone as she stares at me. "You mean you're serious?"

Amelia and Ellie stare too; open-mouthed and wide-eyed from their seats across the table. We're seated around a little table in my basement apartment after stopping at Subway to get some lunch. I'd asked them to come over to hang out since we hadn't done so in a long time, and to break the news to them before too much time had passed, otherwise I was risking their collective wrath. All four of us have been best friends since high school, but Lisa and I had been inseparable since fifth grade.

"Yes. I'm serious," I answer.

I had made sure that I was totally ready for this conversation before even making the phone calls to set it in motion. Step one: I hadn't cried in over a week. Step two: Nicole and I were checking in with each other by phone just to talk and keep an open communication line between us. Step three: I could be in a room with Michael without crying, getting angry or starting an argument.

I feel emotionally stable, and I absolutely need to be before talking to them about this. They are going to come at me from every angle, like master, heavy weight boxers, and I need to have acceptable, sincere answers for them.

They all start talking at once, raising their voices as they try to talk over each other, and I'm glad that my mother has taken Gabey with her and my father to my grandmother's house for the afternoon. All the noise would have freaked him out. It's Lisa, usually the quietest of our group, who eventually dominates.

"Whoa. Let me talk!" she shouts, as far as shouting goes with her, and shocked, Amelia and Ellie clamp their mouths shut, giving Lisa the floor.

Lisa looks at me and says firmly, her expression incredulous, "So, he's married another wife and you're ok with this?"

"Yes," I reply simply, my heart pounding in my chest in response to her intensity.

I can imagine all kinds of things that she might be thinking, but I have prepared by reminding myself to not assume – to just take their questions as they come and to answer them as honestly as I possibly can.

"Why?!" she demands, her face becoming flushed, and I can't tell if she's angry with me or sad for me.

"Your father is ok with this?" Ellie, ever the pragmatist, askes doubtfully. "We might all know and accept that you're a grown, married woman but he doesn't. Did he get in a fight with Michael?"

"I haven't told him yet, just ma and Aunt Pam," I answer.

And Ellie's right. One of the reasons that I had called them over is to try to get their support before I tell my father. If they're on my side, then it will be easier to convince him that Michael isn't a villain.

"Oooh girl," Amelia says, her normal light-heartedness replaced with foreboding. "I can't believe this. I thought Michael was joking all those times when he used to ask us what we thought about polygamy!"

"Me too!" Lisa agrees heatedly and glares at me. "Why are you ok with this?"

They all stare at me again and wait for my response. I know they may not accept it, but I have to be honest. I take a deep breath and begin.

"Ok. Without going too deep. I prayed about it, and I asked God to help me to have peace and happiness with this if this is God's will for me. I also asked God to take it away from me and out of my life if it isn't God's will for me. It's been almost a month since I prayed that prayer, and although I can't say that I'm happy with it yet, I can say that I'm at peace with it, and that I can see the potential for happiness," I answer as forthrightly as I can. "Everything gets better and easier to accept every single day."

Lisa appears resigned at that answer, Ellie shrugs her shoulders noncommittally and nods her head, indicating that she can get on board with that, and Amelia looks skeptical, but also resigned. They each had similar reactions when I'd told them that I had converted to Islam.

I haven't been religious throughout most of my life, and it wasn't until college that I had begun to explore spirituality, which had caused some distance between us at first because of the changes that came with it. I worry a little that revealing this new layer to my relationship with God will be a double whammy and I just hope and pray that they won't find it too hard to accept.

"This is on him," Lisa finally states resentfully. "How could he?! If your father does go after him, I won't try to stop him."

I know she's angry and that she doesn't really mean that. I had been angry too, and I just want to do what I can to help her to not be upset.

"That's not true, though, Li," I say. "Believe me, I was pissed too when he first told me, but he didn't force me to accept this. I chose to."

"He kind of did though," Amelia adds heatedly. "He knows you! He did this and told you after the fact. You two have a baby together. He knows that you won't just divorce him."

"I disagree," Ellie says thoughtfully. "Think about it. We know Michael. He loves her. He wouldn't want her to be in the marriage if she's unhappy. He's not a jerk."

Amelia and Ellie begin to disagree about Michael's character and the nature of men in general while Lisa half-listens, her expression thoughtful, before she asks me, "I get that you prayed about this. And I respect that. But did you pray about it because you wanted to, or because he asked you to?"

"Both," I answer truthfully. "I wasn't able to pray about it at first. I couldn't sleep for a week and I hardly ate, but it got to the point where I had to ask myself what I wanted. Did I want to give this a try, or did I want to get a divorce? To be honest, every day I ask myself this question and it get easier and easier to find happiness."

"But why should you have to work so hard!" Amelia says. "It shouldn't have to get easier and easier; it should be easy. Period. Marriage shouldn't be a struggle. I still think you two were too young to get married anyway."

"Why shouldn't they have to work at it, though?" Ellie asks. "Relationships ain't easy. It takes work and compromise no matter who you're with. It's like anything in life. Like they say, anything worth having is worth working for."

Amelia and Ellie are about to start going back and forth again when Lisa interjects.

"Who is the new wife? Have you met her yet?" Lisa demands.

My stomach flips over nervously. This is the moment of truth that all of the questions have been building up towards and I know instinctively that if I don't handle it carefully it will go completely sideways. Nicole and I had met in college, so they didn't know her that well. Worst case scenario: they won't want to get to know her any better going forward. I have to handle this with the utmost care. I love them, and I love Nicole, so I want them all to love each other.

"Why are you taking so long to answer me?" Lisa asks astutely; it's like she can read my mind sometimes.

"It better not be anybody we know. Islam or no Islam, there's going to be problems if it is," Amelia says hotly.

I swallow in a dry throat and reply, "Well. You know that it wasn't just Michael and I that converted to Islam. You remember our friends from college, right? How they converted at the same time with us too."

"So, it's one of your college friends?" Amelia asks, outraged.

I want to stall, and my mind searches frantically for something that can ease into this revelation smoothly, but I can't think of anything, so I finally say, "It's Nicole."

Their mouths drop open at the same time when I blurt Nicole's name. I watch the fluctuating emotions on their faces as they process it. Shock. Outrage. Anger. Worry. Determination. Resolve.

"I can't believe you're accepting this," Lisa finally says and pushes away from the table to stand up. "I can't accept this. You deserve better. More love. All the love, not half the love."

"Yes!" Amelia agrees whole heartedly.

"I agree, Jo," even Ellie says. "That's a little too much. She's supposed to be your friend."

"I'm not *accepting* this, ladies," I respond calmy. "I'm *choosing* this. I've chosen this. And it's not half the love. When he's with me; it's our love, our whole love. And when he's with her, it's theirs – it's totally separate from me. The best way to think of it is that there is one love and two wives that share in that love."

"How is that even possible?!" Lisa asks dismissively.

"I don't know. But that's how it feels," I answer.

"You can't tell me that you don't get jealous. I know you," Lisa continues, starting to pace back and forth across the room as if she's thinking aloud and not talking directly to me. "Where is he now? In Boston? With her? I'm pissed for you! We should drive up there right now."

"Drive up there is do what? Tell him how mad we are?" Amelia says, laughing dryly and falling into her natural tendency to make jokes. "She's already said that she's chosen this, Lisa."

It amazes me how Lisa is giving voice to all of the feelings that I had initially had, and it just reaffirms our connection. From the moment when we were 11 years old, and she'd come over to my house to get a copy of the Janet Jackson tape that I had dubbed for her we'd done just about everything together. College and the changes that we were both going through at that time had created a little bit of a gulf between us, and I'd almost lost her when I'd converted to Islam. I don't want to lose her friendship to this. I have to say all that I can to calm her down and to help her to at least find peace with this, like I had. She stops pacing and stands by the glass doors to look out at the backyard.

"Lisa, can you please just try to understand," I say, standing up and walking over to stand beside her. "I'm hearing everything that you're saying. And you're right, I do get jealous sometimes, but I'm working on it. Like Ellie said, that's what relationships are all about: about working out the problems that come up. And I promise you, if it gets to a point where I can't be happy and be able to live my life fully, I will leave. But I won't just walk away without at least trying."

She looks over at me and smiles slightly.

"You're too nice," she says begrudgingly.

I think I've finally got through and I smile back. I grab her hand and hold it, nudging her shoulder with mine. She nudges me back and hugs me, sighing deeply.

"Group hug!" Amelia shouts and grabs Ellie's hand, pulling her up from the table and tugging her over to us.

She flings her arms around us, pulling Ellie into the hug, and we all half laugh, half cry together. I'm so relieved and happy to be surrounded by their love and support that I offer a silent prayer of gratitude.

"So, does this mean that you all are going to give this a chance to work? I might need your help telling dad," I say as we release each other.

"I don't know about getting involved when you face your father with this, but I suppose I won't cut you off completely," Lisa teases and goes back to the table to finish drinking her iced tea.

"I don't think I can be any help, but I definitely want to be there when you tell him!" Amelia says, rubbing her hands together expectantly, anticipating drama.

"Just call me, Jo, I'll be there if you want me to," Ellie says, her steady, relaxed demeanor will most definitely be helpful.

We collectively sigh with relief and sit back down at the table to finish eating our sandwiches.

"Thanks for putting us through all that," Lisa says sarcastically before taking a bite of her turkey sub.

We all laugh and fall back into our flow.

"I know, right!" Amelia says and pokes her tuna sandwich with her finger. "My sandwich is all soggy now. You owe me a fresh sandwich."

"Mine is fine," Ellie says and bites into her meatball marinara sub.

"Mine is too," I say and pick up my tuna sub to take a bite.

The conversation shifts to how much better D'Angelo's subs are than Subway and I try not to smile too hard as I listen to them go back and forth. I'm so happy that I can hardly contain myself.

Our friendships have lasted between seven to ten years so far. We've grown up together, and we had come into adulthood together. I can't imagine the rest of my life without them being a part of it. The love and respect we have for one another gives me hope that my friendship with Nicole will survive this too.

Chapter Nine

Daddy's Girl

I finally have a day to relax. Michael's graduation has come and gone without a hitch, summer has begun so the workload has slowed down at my job, Gabey is weaned and more independent so I have my body back and less stress chasing him around, and I'm beginning to feel like I'm gaining a pretty good understanding about the deen.

It's been six months since my shahadah, and I no longer feel like such a newbie when I go to the masjid. In that time, I've read the entire English translation of the Quran from cover to cover, I've read just about every book that I can find about the basic pillars of Islam, and I feel good that I've memorized the last twelve surahs of the Quran in both English and Arabic so I no longer have to read from a printout during salaat.

The sky is clear, and the sun is bright as I sit out in the backyard on one of the lawn chairs reading about the importance of dawah in Islam while Gabriel shuffles around in the grass on the little scooter my parents had just bought for him. Michael is visiting with his mother and brother in the Bronx this weekend which is nice for him. Gabey and I had stayed home because he plans on telling them about Nicole.

My mind drifts to how that might be going when I hear the screen door creak open, and slam shut. I look up to see my dad striding deliberately towards me and judging by the expression on his face, he is far from happy. My mother follows a few seconds behind him and hurries to keep up with him as he stomps across the yard.

"Joseph, calm down," she says. "It's not what you think."

He reaches me and when I meet his gaze, looking up into a face that is so much like my own that all of his friends call me a little female version of Joe (hence my nickname), I know that he has found out about the marriage.

"Is it true?!" he shouts loudly, hovering over me; he is so angry that it seems like it's simmering off his skin in waves of heat.

Gabey looks up from his scooter curiously at the sound of my father's raised voice so my mother, just as in tuned to Gabriel's moods as I am, walks over to him and picks him up from the scooter.

"Hey, Nana's baby! Ready to eat-eat?" she says cheerily and sends me a covert, apologetic look as she goes back towards the house.

I'm left to wonder who has spilled the beans and to face my father alone.

"Yes," I answer calmly, closing my book and putting it down on the table beside me carefully, like being cornered by a bear (a great big papa bear) and not wanting to make any sudden moves.

"Wh-the! I! This m-! Um gonna," he sputters furiously and turns away from me to pace around in circles, rubbing the top of his head in frustration.

I sit still and silent while he processes my answer. His expression fluctuates between rage and disappointment as his mind grapples with his emotions and I silently thank God that Michael is miles away. He punches the palm of his hand, then stops pacing long enough to glare at me before turning away again and pacing over to the wooden fence encircling our backyard. He stands at the fence for several minutes, his shoulders tense and his back facing me, and when I see his shoulders slump and his head drop down towards his chest, I realize that the worst is over and that he is almost ready to talk to me.

As a daddy's girl through and through, my eyes fill with tears at the disappointment that I know he is now experiencing. My whole life so far has been spent trying to make him and my mother happy and proud of me and I instinctively understand how difficult it is for him to approve of this. I hadn't even thought about what I actually wanted out of life until I had gone off to college and had felt what it was like to live life on my own. After twenty three years of living in my father's presence I know that this isn't what he wants for me.

I get up and walk over to him. He tenses visibly when I reach him, but I lay my head against his arm anyway, waiting for him to relax and to speak. When he finally does his voice is thick with emotion.

"I could hurt him. I really could. I knew that this was coming when you told me you were becoming Muslim," he says, but the fury is gone from his voice.

As a child of the 1960's, my father knows about Islam, but primarily about the Nation of Islam's version and how polygamy had been an accepted practice by many of its members.

"He broke his promise to me. He said that he would take good care of you. Now look," my father says and turns to face me, his dark brown eyes filled with pain.

"He didn't break his promise, though, daddy," I explain. "He's still taking good care of me. He's gotten his degree, he's got a steady, good-paying job, and we're saving up to get our own place. Nothing has changed other than now there's another person building with the two of us towards our goals."

He shakes his head defiantly and says, "Why isn't one wife enough? That's what the Bible says: one wife! That's what's right and best for everybody."

"Why, dad? Why is that what is best and right? The Bible doesn't say that anywhere," I reply quietly, pushing back gently and not wanting to upset him but trying to get him to listen to reason rather than to be led by his emotions. "Michael still loves me, and I still love him. He's just added another person to our family to love."

He's quiet for a minute, letting that sink in.

"And it's Nicole, right? You know your Aunt Pam can't hold water . . . running that mouth of hers . . . She said he married Nicole right after Christmas," my father probes, staring into my eyes and searching for any signs of pain in them.

"Yeah, it's Nicole. It was hard at first to accept that, but I prayed about it, and she and I have even prayed together. It's a work in progress, but it's progressing. And I'm ok, dad. I really am," I respond honestly, meeting his gaze and placing a reassuring hand on his arm.

"This isn't what I wanted for you, honey," he says and his voice breaks with tears.

My own eyes well up again and I can hardly keep it together – my father never cries. I hug him around the waist and lay my head against his chest.

"This isn't what I envisioned for my life either, dad. But God plans things for us that we don't always understand or even like sometimes, until we get to see the wisdom in it. Think about yourself and wanting to play professional basketball. That's what you had envisioned, but you got injured and couldn't go on to fulfill that dream. God had other plans for you, though. You raised a beautiful family; you've been a role model in our whole extended family and in the neighborhood – your life is still good. And that's how I feel. I may not be Michael's only wife, but he loves me, he's committed to me, and we're still trying to build a family that will be good and strong; something that we can look back on one day and be happy about," I say.

He hugs me tightly and pats my head like he used to when I was little.

"What did I do to get such a child," he finally says.

"What did I do to get such a great father?" I respond back as he lets me go and takes a deep breath.

He grins and pats my head again, then squints his eyes and says soberly, "I won't hurt him. But I'll be watching him. Each and every step, every day, every year, I'll be watching and on the ready."

I shake my head and smile, thankful that he is at least willing to give this a chance but mindful that he never says anything in vain. I just hope, for all of our sakes, that this works out.

Chapter Ten

Her.

Gabriel is fast asleep in his crib. The night is warm, so I have the windows open instead of putting on the AC. Crickets sing their songs from the bushes in the backyard and the white light of a full moon bounces off the glass doors. It's Friday night, and Michael is on his way home for the weekend.

The three of us have agreed that it's best for Michael to stay in Boston during the week to make it less expensive for him to commute back and forth to work, so he and his best friend Marcus have kept the apartment that they had been sharing during the school year. To keep the schedules fair, Michael takes turns spending the weekends here in Providence or at Nicole's apartment with her. This weekend he's going to be here with us, and I can't wait to see him.

I've showered and flat-ironed my hair, letting it hang loose past my shoulders, and I'm wearing the new night gown that I'd bought at the mall earlier. I have even layered the scent of my white citrus body wash with the matching lotion and body spray in anticipation of his arrival. I give myself one more look in the mirror while I wait for him to arrive. I've finally lost the extra baby weight so I'm feeling pretty good about myself.

Headlights flash across the room as Michael's cab drives up to the house, letting me know that he's here, so I hurry over to the bed to get in position. I pick up my book, open to the last page that I had been reading, and lean back against the headboard, stretching out my legs in front of me and trying to read but I'm totally and completely not interested in reading about the particulars of Arabic grammar – not tonight.

The back door opens and closes quietly, and my heart skips a beat. This coming October will be our third-year anniversary and I still get this excited, I'm-so-glad-he's-here feeling whenever he comes home or calls. He descends the stairs quietly, mindful of the hour and of the darkness of the house.

He grins when he sees me and drops his bags onto the couch before walking over to me. He's wearing a white t-shirt and jeans under an unbuttoned plaid, short sleeved collared shirt and he looks like he's still a college student. I get up to hug him, standing on my tiptoes, and my arms barely reach around his neck. He laughs and picks me up off the floor easily, holding me close to his chest and burying his face against my neck.

"You smell good," he says against my skin.

I can't speak. He pulls away to kiss me gently and gingerly places me back onto the bed. His eyes are sparkling brightly, and he takes off his collared shirt, letting it drop to the floor, before he leans over me, placing a hand on each side of my hips and getting ready to kiss me again when I see it: a hickey! A bright red splotch stands out starkly against the honey brown of his skin on the side of his neck and my mouth drops open in shock.

I immediately push away from him and glare angrily into his eyes. He is so completely confused and surprised by my reaction that he falls face forward onto the bed in the spot that I have just vacated.

"What's wrong?" he demands; befuddled frustration is evident in every inch of his face.

I still can't speak, but this time it's because I don't know what to say. This shouldn't be such a shock to me, but it is. With Nicole living in Boston and me in Providence, she and I hardly ever see each other since she started her internship, so I don't think about the intimacy aspect of their relationship that much. And when I do, I'm always able to reason my way out of an emotional tantrum by focusing on my relationship with him rather than speculating about hers. But this. This is a bright, blatant reminder of just how much she and I are sharing.

I get up from the bed and walk over to the bathroom where my robe is hanging on the back of the door. I quickly put it on and tie the belt tightly around my waist before returning to stand in front of him with my arms crossed over my chest. He is sitting up on the edge of the bed, watching me with the same look of confusion, and he heaves a sigh of frustration when I plop down angrily beside him.

"What is wrong?" he asks again, emphasizing each word deliberately.

"Uh - have you had a look in the mirror lately?" I retort, equally frustrated.

He immediately gets up and walks over to the bureau to look in the mirror. He checks his face and head, then his neck, and understanding washes over his features. He turns around to face me and leans his back against the bureau, hanging his head. He looks embarrassed and becomes sheepish. Now he doesn't have anything to say.

"Well?" I demand, furious that he hadn't paid enough attention to himself to have provided me with some kind of warning or heads up.

"Well, what? Am I supposed to apologize, Jo? This is a part of marriage," Michael says defensively, but with the same sheepish expression on his face.

"Maybe not apologize, but you can at least be humbler about it. How would you feel if I came home with a hickey on my neck?" I ask, also defensive.

"That's ridiculous, Joanna. It's not nearly the same thing," he says and returns to the bed, angrily taking off his sneakers.

"Yes, it is. On a human-to-human level, it's exactly the same. Imagine that the Quran says a woman can take up to four husbands. How would you feel if you came home to find me with a glaring hickey on my neck? Not good, I bet," I say.

Sighing heavily with exasperation, he looks up at the ceiling and throws his arms in the air before looking back at me and saying, "Are we really going to do this right now, Jo?"

His eyes plead with me to relax and he leans towards me, but I move back and answer, "Yes we are."

Fed up, he straightens and sighs again, angrily this time. He takes off his jeans and drops them to the floor then removes his t-shirt. Stripped down to his normal sleepwear of undershirt and boxers, he climbs into the bed. I scoot to the opposite side and wait for him to respond.

"I'm too tired to have this conversation, Joanna," he says and turns over onto his side angrily, with his back towards me. "If you really want to go on about 'what ifs,' which as you know you're not even supposed to do in Islam, then we'll have to talk tomorrow. I've been working all day, I wasn't able to make it to jumuah, I had to work at the masjid after work, then of course I had to go through a whole thing with Nicole about my leaving for the weekend and she and I not having spent any time together during her weekend – I'm exhausted."

"Uh. I beg to differ. That thing didn't just magically appear on your neck! You spent *some* kind of time together because it wasn't there when I last saw you!" I retort indignantly and lay down on my side of the bed, putting my back to him as well. "And like you always love to tell me, this is your responsibility, Michael. You chose this lifestyle too. You chose it first, so you're even more responsible than she and I are. I worked all day too. And then I came home to take care of our son, who you hardly see anymore. So please. If you're going to go to bed angry, be angry at yourself, not me."

We lay there in the bed, both of us clutching to our self-righteous indignation at the other, and it was as if there was a third person right there in the bed between us. Nicole. My co-wife.

Chapter Eleven

Him.

"Come on, Joanna! We haven't seen you in weeks! It's a shame that we have to corner you at your job after work just to get you to come out with us," Lisa says as she leans over my desk and snatches the pen out of my hand. "I know Aunt Pam won't mind if you're a couple of hours late."

"I can't. I really can't. Michael and I had an argument and he's supposed to be coming in town early so we can talk," I say, although I'm not looking forward to it at all.

Amelia huffs dismissively and says, "He can wait. Let him sit around waiting for you this time. We promise not to keep you too long, besides, you look like you need to talk to us first. Trouble in Paradise?"

She laughs at her own joke, as she often does, and nudges Lisa for a laugh. Lisa rolls her eyes.

"Don't blow us off. And I agree with Amelia, you should talk to us first. What happened?" Lisa asks, suddenly more interested in hearing what the argument was about than in getting me to join them for happy hour.

"I'm not blowing you off, but I really don't want to go to anybody's happy hour," I object firmly.

"Fine. Then to my house," Lisa says begrudgingly. "My mother is away this weekend, so we'll have the house to ourselves."

I really don't want to make matters worse than they already are by being late going home when I know that it wasn't easy for Michael to re-arrange his schedule, but it had been weeks since we'd had a girl's night, and no matter what anybody says, there is nothing like the healing power of being around sister-friends.

I'm about to try to convince them to do this tomorrow night instead when my cell phone chimes, alerting me to a text message. It's Michael. Lisa and Amelia are watchful as I read the text.

I'm sorry babe. Can't get away until later, Imam Qadhi needs me to fill in for him on the panel discussion. Will get the late T tonight or the first one in the morning. Love you. Salaams.

I sigh heavily and text him back, then I text my mother to tell her that I'll be going over to Lisa's for a few hours and asking her to watch Gabey until I get home. Lisa and Amelia can tell from my expression that I'm disappointed, but they don't say or ask anything.

"All right. Let's go," I tell them, trying to sound cheerful. "I need this. Michael's running late and may not even get back until the morning."

Lisa and Amelia high-five each other and grin happily.

"Fun-ness!" Amelia says.

I shut down my computer and pull my work bag and purse out of my lower desk drawer. Everyone else in the office has left for the day so I have to lock up.

"I'll meet you two outside," I say as I lock my desk.

"Ok, I'll order some take out from the car so we can pick it up on the way," Lisa says as she follows Amelia through the heavy front doors.

Once they're gone, I let myself feel the emotions that are boiling just beneath the surface of my psyche. Not just disappointment, but rejection, anger and neglect. It's been two weeks since the argument and since I've seen him. Granted, I've been distant, but he has too. We never did finish the talk about how he would feel if the tables were turned, and we had essentially just passed the rest of our weekend together holding a grudge against each other.

I hurry upstairs to make sure that all of the lights have been turned off up there, and then return to the bottom floor of the building to turn off the lights down there before exiting and locking the heavy wooden doors behind me. I walk over to Lisa's car and open the back door to climb in.

"Can you turn it down?" I almost have to shout; the music is blasting.

Lisa and Amelia laugh at the same time, most likely having turned up the music just to get a rise out of me, and immediately begin to mock me playfully.

"You kids turn that darned music down, ya hear me!" Amelia says, pointing her finger at me scoldingly.

"That music will rot ya brain," Lisa says in a high-pitched voice which is supposed to be her impersonation of an old woman.

They laugh again and Lisa grins and says, "Don't be such an old lady. Sheesh. You're only twenty-three."

She turns the music down a notch, and I roll my eyes, shaking my head with a smile – but they sound like my mother. My life completely changed when Gabriel was born so at the age of 21, I had to take on the responsibility of being a mom and a wife. I didn't realize that my behavior was more like that of a 33-year-old than a twenty three year old, but my mother had; and Lisa, Amelia and Ellie have.

"So, what happened?" Amelia asks, turning down the volume of the music further and twisting around in the passenger seat to look at me. "What was this argument about?"

My face gets hot with embarrassment, and I anticipate what their reactions are going to be, but I need to speak aloud to somebody about this if I'm going to get past it. I explain the entire situation to them from start to finish, including how he'd left that Sunday night, still angry, and that he and I haven't talked or communicated other than texting about bills and household stuff that couldn't be avoided since then. Lisa has reached the Chinese restaurant to pick up our takeout by the time I'm done telling them everything.

To my surprise, they're both quiet. Lisa had parked the car and had turned around to look at me too, and they just sat there staring at me, as if waiting for me to tell them more.

I finally have to ask them, "Well???? What do you think?"

They look at each other, bewildered, and turn back to face me. Lisa speaks first.

"Well. I mean. That's part of it, right? It's not like they have a platonic relationship, do they?" she asks sincerely.

"That's what I was thinking," Amelia says. "I mean, I understand that you are hurt to have seen evidence of it, but Jo, this is what you're in. Why do you think we objected so much about it?"

They are right, of course, but I want them to be on my side of this. I didn't expect them to side with him!

"I know that, but he should have hidden it, or given me a heads up or something! Or he should tell her to not leave marks on him! If it were me, and if I had come home with some other man's mark on me, I can't even imagine how he'd react!" I fume, begging them with my eyes to side with me.

"That's true, but then you would have to say the same thing to him that we're saying to you now: that he chose this," Lisa says. "We support you in this choice, Jo, because you asked us to and because we love you. So, as your friends, we have to tell you honestly what we think is the right thing to do in this situation."

Amelia nods and adds, "It sucks though. What a way to spoil the mood."

Defeated, I sigh and stare back at them.

"So, do you think I owe him an apology?" I ask incredulously.

"No," Lisa says vehemently.

"Absolutely not," Amelia says at the same instant.

"You might have reacted badly, but if you two are going to work it out then you have to do just that. You have the right to be upset, but what are you two going to *do* about it?" Lisa asks rhetorically.

"Yes!" Amelia agrees. "He brought you into this. Now he has to deal with what comes with it! I sure would never let my husband marry another wife! I don't know how you do it."

I sigh again, feeling a little better for having talked about it and gotten some insights from them, but still unsure of what to do. I expected to vent and to have them qualify all of my points, but instead they have given me some food for thought. I take this as a sign that God does want plural marriage for me, or at the very least, that there are life lessons that I need to learn from this situation.

"I'll be right back," Lisa says and hops out of the car to get the Chinese food.

Once she's gone, Amelia asks, "Do you still want to stay married like this? I mean, that really sucks. I don't think I could handle knowing that my man was having relations with another woman on the regular."

I have to think about it for a minute before I can respond.

"Yeah. I mean, I think so. But the sex part . . . I don't even know if I want it ever again," I answer honestly.

The past two weeks have given me lots of time to stew over the real reason why I was so angry at the sight of the evidence of Michael and Nicole's intimate relationship and that is because deep down inside, I still don't want to share him. Even after all of the praying, and all of the good days and nice talks between Nicole and I, I don't want to actually share him or his love with her or anyone else. Tears prick my eyes as I realize that if this is going to work, I have to not only embrace sharing him, but support and encourage sharing him so that we can all have healthy, productive relationships with one another.

Amelia notices my tears before I can look away and nods her head compassionately, making a sad face before reaching over to give me a hug but her seatbelt stops her. We laugh as she is jerked back into her seat and give each other an air hug instead. Lisa opens the back door to put the bag of food beside me at that moment.

"What are you two laughing about?" she asks incredulously. "This is not a laughable subject."

She gets back into the driver's seat and starts up the car as Amelia fills her in.

"Geez," she says with a frown and jokes dryly. "That definitely is a pickle."

"Break it down for us. What exactly is it that makes it so hard for you?" Amelia asks.

"I don't know," I answer, not sure if I should go into too much detail about it.

"Think about it," Lisa says and glances at me through the rearview mirror as she drives. "I mean, there's got to be a reason. I can think of the reason why I would be pissed and it's because if I caught Allen with a hickey on his neck it would be because he had cheated. Do you feel like Michael is cheating on you when he's with her?"

I think about it and respond, "No, not really. I guess I just feel jealous. I don't understand how he could want or allow her to touch him so intimately and still love me."

"But men say all the time that sex isn't connected to love with them the same way that it is for us. That's probably why mean cheat so much more than women do, though," Amelia says, adding the last sentence thoughtfully.

"Jealousy is understandable," Lisa says. "I think we all deal with that on some level, even in monogamous relationships. Maybe if you just tune out the fact that they even, you know . . . then you'll be able to avoid feeling any jealousy about it."

"But tuning it out is work," Amelia interjects. "You don't want to have to live the rest of your life pretending that your husband isn't having sex with his other wife, do you?"

"Blunt enough?" Lisa replies with dry sarcasm to Amelia's response, but Amelia's point is so accurate that I have to take a minute to think about that.

And I realize that I don't. I don't want to have to spend the rest of my life pretending that Nicole and Michael don't have a full, complete marriage. And I don't think that God wants that for me either. If the Quran says that this is permissible, then there has to be a graceful and merciful solution to what I'm feeling.

We reach Lisa's mother's house and climb out of the car. I close the back door and I'm about to turn to follow them up the driveway when I hear someone shout from across the street.

"Hey, Lisa! Hey Amelia! Is that Joanna with you?"

I turn around to find Joshua, a former classmate of ours from high school, jogging over to us. He reaches me first, Lisa and Amelia are already halfway up the driveway, and before I can react, he hugs me tightly, lifting me up off my feet briefly, and setting me back down. He grins widely at me and takes a step back to look at me.

"Still cute as a button and still the same height as you were freshman year. I'm convinced you have hobbit in your blood. And what's this? You're a Muslim?" he asks curiously, lifting the edge of my headscarf and letting it drop back to my shoulder.

"Yes," I answer awkwardly, embarrassed by the attention and surprised by the sight of him. "For a few months now – Six months."

He's still as handsome as he was in high school, if not more so now that he's older. From the look of him he must not have stopped playing basketball regularly and he's just as friendly as I remember him.

"I forgot to tell you that Joshua lives across the street," Lisa says as she reaches us.

He hugs her and Amelia before returning his attention to me.

"Wow," he says. "A Muslim. I played ball in the Emirates for a few years. I'm surprised but not surprised. You were always so nice. Islam gets a bad rap here in the states. I hope you haven't been harassed or anything. But wait, you're married, right?"

"Our food is getting cold, Josh. You're going to have to catch up another time," Lisa says impatiently and grabs my arm.

He follows us up the driveway and asks, "Whatcha got in that bag? Let me have some."

"No, now get outta here," Lisa says teasingly, but stone-faced and dropping the "r" in "here" to exaggerate the Rhode Island accent that we all still have, Josh more than any of us.

"You're wrong for that," he replies and laughs as she unlocks the door, but it sounds more like, "Yaw wrong faw dat."

"Bye, Josh," Amelia says.

"Seeya, Josh," Lisa says with a playful grin and begins to close the door.

"Night, Josh, nice seeing you," I say through a crack before the door closes.

Lisa laughs wickedly and thoroughly when the door clicks shut loudly, making us all laugh with her.

"I can hear you," Josh yells from beyond the closed door with laughter in his voice. "I'll be back."

He said "I'll be back" with an Arnold Schwarzenegger accent.

Once we stop laughing, we remember the food and walk into the kitchen to put down our purses, and I my work bag and purse, down while Lisa gets plates and utensils. Amelia gets some cups from the cupboard and I check the refrigerator for something to drink. It's like no time has passed since we were in high school when our daily routine was school, work and/or practice (Lisa and I: track; Amelia and Ellie: cheerleading) and raiding the refrigerator at one of our parents' homes.

"He looked awfully curious about you," Lisa says as she places plates and serving spoons on the table.

"And what was up with that hug?" Amelia exclaims. "He never hugs me like that."

"Didn't you have a crush on him in high school?" Lisa asks and removes the paper cartons of fried rice and lo mein from the large paper bag.

"I thought we all did?" I ask and we laugh some more together.

"You're right, you're right. We all did," Lisa says with a grin. "Well, it looks like he's crushing on you now."

"And the timing couldn't be better if you're looking for some revenge," Amelia teases.

"I couldn't. Not ever. That's part of why this is so hard. I could hardly take Josh hugging me, never mind anything else. It just hurts that it doesn't seem to be the same way for Michael," I reply.

"Ask him," Lisa says. "If you can handle the answer. Maybe it's not as easy for him to compartmentalize in this area as you think it is."

I hadn't thought of that. Maybe the way forward is an honest conversation about the nature of our intimate relationship now that he has two wives instead of just one.

We spoon food onto our plates in comfortable silence and I feel like a weight has lifted from my heart. This is more than what I had needed to decompress. Much more. Nothing like a girl's night to put things into perspective. Now I can go home and pray about this with an open heart.

Chapter Twelve

Us

Buoyed by the energy generated during girl's night, I walk into my parents' house several hours later with a smile on my face and with laughter in my heart. Lisa had dropped me off and had promised that we would all do it again soon, and maybe next time cook something together. The house is dark and quiet when I enter, and since my mother had already texted me to let me know that Gabriel was fast asleep for the night with her and my dad upstairs in their bedroom, I go down to the basement to make Isha prayer and to get ready for bed myself.

I'm surprised to see Michael sitting on our bed in the dark when I reach the bottom of the stairs and, startled, I nearly jump out of my skin. He hadn't called or texted to let me know that he'd arrived, and my mother hadn't mentioned that he was home either.

"As Salaamu Alaikum," I say with surprise and put my work bag and my purse down on the couch before taking off my shoes and walking over to him. "When did you get here?"

"About an hour ago," he responds curtly, neglecting to return the salaams to me and thus putting me on the defensive, my smile fades away.

"Why didn't you text me? I was at Lisa's. I would have come home sooner," I say as I take off my jacket and hang it up in our makeshift closet.

"Why didn't you tell me that you were going over to Lisa's when you texted me earlier?" he asks and turns on the lamp on the bedside table, giving me a full view of his frowning face as if I couldn't already tell that he was angry from the tone of his voice.

"I didn't know that I had to. What, I can't go anywhere without telling you now?" I ask, letting my frustration get the better of me before reminding myself that we are supposed to be smoothing things over, not making things worse. "I'm sorry, I shouldn't have said that."

I sigh deeply and sit down on the bed beside him, willing myself to let down my defenses. He glares at me for a few seconds before his features finally smooth out, and he sighs deeply too.

"And I apologize for not giving you the greeting. Walaikum As Salaam," he says, his tone much gentler, and he holds out his hand towards me.

I put my hand in his and reply, "It's ok."

We sit there in silence for a few more seconds before he finally asks, "Did you have fun?"

I can tell that he is trying to start over and I'm willing to meet him halfway.

"Yeah. It was a lot of fun. We ordered in Chinese food, and talked, and reminisced about when we were younger. It was really nice," I say, trying to share some of the positive energy with him despite the lurking tension between us.

"I'm glad you had a nice time," he says. "I should have called or let you know that I was on my way. I just assumed that you would be here."

He sounds a little hurt when he says that last sentence. I can understand his hurt, but I'm a little hurt too and it takes an effort not to let that hurt dominate the conversation. He may be hurt that I wasn't here when he arrived, but I was hurt because he'd said he was coming home early but had let work take priority over us. The bottom line is that we have to compromise, and that this is the tough work that we are going to have to put into our relationship if we want it to be healthy. I extend an olive branch by explaining my actions to him.

"I was frustrated after you texted and said that you weren't going to make it home early, and they stopped by after work to ask me to hang out with them. I needed the time to just relax and to not worry about anything," I say.

"I know," he responds.

Another lingering silence. We hold each other's hands, both of us with our heads bowed and looking down at our entwined fingers, my dark brown skin against his lighter, honey brown. Then he turns towards me and faces me. I lift my head to meet his gaze.

"So, I've thought about what you said that night and you're right, I would have been just as mad if the situation had been turned around the other way around," he admits quietly. "I should have been more sensitive to your feelings."

I smile slightly, thankful for the admission, and respond, "And I should have handled myself better rather than that. I let the anger and jealousy I felt from seeing the evidence of your physical relationship with Nicole get the best of me."

He smiles back and says, "At least we now know that we have to be prepared for things that might come up that are difficult to manage. I was thinking that we should start having family meetings. To be able to talk to each regularly and say whatever we might be going through. All three of us are working, we all get stressed, and we're all getting used to these new dynamics between us – with meetings we can try to work things out before they become too big to handle without a blow up."

I think about that for a few seconds. My expression must clearly reveal my uncertainty because he immediately continues.

"It's just a thought," he says. "We're in this together. I've been thinking a lot about this. Many people believe that polygyny can't work because it stirs up too many destructive emotions: jealousy, possessiveness, envy . . . But we're building here. We're creating a foundation for a family rooted in peace and righteousness. We have to stay focused on what builds us up, not on what tears us down."

I meet his gaze and think about that. The thought comes to my mind about how some people think that a second wife has the potential to be a homewrecker, but based on what Michael has just said, it doesn't have to be that way. It might be that way for some people, but it doesn't have to be that way for us.

"Let's both just agree to not shut down on each other anymore. Can we do that at least?" he asks.

I nod and reply, "Yes. I can agree to that."

He hugs me and holds me close to him. We stay like that for several long moments before he reclines backwards onto the bed, bringing me with him and making room for me to nestle into his side. I lay my head upon his shoulder and my smile returns. We can do this. I know we can. As long as we stay committed to each other and focused on our faith – focused on creating a family that's meant to last – we will thrive.

Chapter Thirteen

Autumn

Leaves are beginning to change color so the treeline against the horizon passes by in golds, reds and browns as I drive myself home today after work. This is my second favorite time of the year. The air is getting cool again, and everything seems to slow down as people start preparing for the encroaching winter.

The angelic sound of the recitation by my favorite Qari flows towards me in gentle waves from the CD player, surrounding me with a feeling of serenity. I whisper, al hamdulilah as a familiar verse touches my heart, then I repeat the verse silently in my head, first in Arabic, then in English, trying to commit it to memory.

Inna almuslimeena walmuslimatiwalmu/mineena walmu/minati walqaniteenawalqanitati wassadiqeena wassadiqatiwassabireena wassabiratiwalkhashiAAeena walkhashiAAatiwalmutasaddiqeena walmutasaddiqatiwassa-imeena wassa-imatiwalhafitheena furoojahum walhafithatiwaththakireena Allaha katheeran waththakiratiaAAadda Allahu lahum maghfiratan waajran AAatheema

Indeed, the Muslim men and Muslim women, the believing men and believing women, the obedient men and obedient women, the truthful men and truthful women, the patient men and patient women, the humble men and humble women, the charitable men and charitable women, the fasting men and fasting women, the men who guard their private parts and the women who do so, and the men who remember Allah often and the women who do so - for them Allah has prepared forgiveness and a great reward.

The verse is from Surat Al-'Aĥzāb, Chapter 33, Verse 35.

I reflect upon the meaning with renewed gratitude as I think about my life and the changes of the past few months. There have been bumps in the road, and I do not doubt that there will be more in the future, but my path is clearer than it's ever been. The seed that was planted in the spring is now ready for harvest, and although it might not be the biggest or the prettiest fruit, it is ripe with promise.

So much has changed in the past six months. I think about how much closer we are to completing the foundation for a family unit based on the principals of Islam, belief, obedience, truth, patience, humility, charity, self-restraint and modesty. Michael has been commuting between Rhode Island and Massachusetts as planned, and everything is falling into place. He and I talk, and listen, more and better than before; and we've both kept our word to not shut down on each other when difficult issues arise. He, Nicole and I have been having family meetings, mainly to coordinate "the family budget," but the meetings have also been good for us as a unit, and we can actually laugh and relax around one another during them. I received a raise at my job, and we found a great price for a rental, so I've been able to move out of my parents' house. Gabey is turning two years old tomorrow, and this will be the first full family gathering since our plural marriage began.

Michael and Nicole will be driving in from Boston tonight, Michael's family is driving down from New York in the morning, my parents, Aunt Pam and my siblings, and my aunts, uncles and cousins who still live in Providence and surrounding towns will all be together for the first time and celebrating this occasion with us in our very first home of our own.

I pull into the driveway, park my little blue Taurus in front of the garage, and take a minute to look over at our first home. It's a rental, and nothing fancy, but it's perfect. Nestled between two large Elm trees on Elgin Street, it's got a working two car garage, it's brown with gold trim and gold shutters around the windows, there are two floors, two bathrooms and three bedrooms, and the living room is big enough for us to convert half of it into a musalla.

Aunt Pam still watches Gabey for me when I'm at work and I remember that she has an outing with her book club tonight, so I hurry out of the car and jog over to the front door. Gabriel is sitting in front of the t.v. watching Bob the Builder on Nick Jr. when I enter the living room. He turns around at the sound of the door closing behind me and smiles and runs over to me when he sees me.

"Mama home!" he shouts excitedly, and I pick him up as soon as he reaches me, kissing his cheeks and squeezing him tightly.

"Hey my baby! As Salaamu Alaikum! How was your day?" I ask, holding him and looking into his beautiful, cherub-like face.

"Slaam alikum," he says, still smiling and rubbing my cheek affectionately. "Aunt Pam in kit-shen. Aunt Pam get cookies."

I laugh happily and reply, "Oh, yeah! What kind of cookies?"

He's been talking much more lately and everything he says delights me, especially the words that I can't understand. It took a little while for me to figure out that kit-shen means kitchen in Gabey-talk, and he was not amused when I laughed the first few times when he said it. Aunt Pam waves from the kitchen where she's standing behind the breakfast bar putting Oreo cookies into a baggie.

"Bwoun cookies," he says with a smile.

He's been learning his colors, so I know that "bwoun" is his best pronunciation of "brown."

"Mmmm. Yummy. What a nice auntie you have. Hey, Auntie," I say and put Gabriel down so he can go and get his "bwoun" cookies.

"Hey, sweetie," she replies with a smile and hands Gabriel the baggie as she steps across the threshold separating the kitchen from the living room.

She picks up her pocketbook and backpack from the sofa and then comes over to give me a hug.

"I gotta run, honey. We're off to Foxwoods tonight so I have to go home so I can get my glam on," she says followed by her loud, throaty laugh and a "pretty girl" pose before picking up Gabriel and hugging him tightly.

I laugh with her and reply, "Ok. Be good! Foxwoods better watch out!"

"You know it. All the time," she says with a wink and heads for the door. "See you tomorrow big boy! For your birthday party!"

"Slaam alikum, Aunt Pam," Gabriel says, distracted by the television.

Once she's gone, Gabriel settles back down in front of the t.v. to finish watching his show, and I drop my purse and my work bag onto the armchair by the front window take off my jacket and shoes. I put my shoes on the low rack by the front door, and my jacket onto one of the four hooks on the wall above it before looking around at the living room happily.

There are still a few boxes that need to be unpacked but overall, we're pretty much moved in. Thanks to family members and friends, every room is furnished, and we didn't have to buy much of anything, mostly blankets and towels and dishes. Late afternoon sunlight adds a touch of gold to everything, and I silently thank Allah for His blessings. I'd made my Asr prayer at work, so I go into the kitchen to check the pantry and the storage closet to make sure that I have all that we need for Gabey's party tomorrow.

Michael and Nicole are supposed to be bringing Gabey's tricycle and the birthday gift bags for the kids that will be here so that is done. Mom, Aunt Pam, and some of my Aunts on my dad's side will be bringing dishes of food to add to the hot dogs and hamburgers that we'll be cooking on the grill, and as I check the shelves in the pantry and in the storage closet it looks like we have everything else that we'll need. Paper plates and plastic utensils: check. Charcoal and lighter fluid: check. Trash bags, potato chips, boxed juices and bottles of water: check. All I need to do now is to make sure that the tables and chairs are set up in the back yard.

Because Michael and Nicole will be here in about an hour, I decide to start cooking dinner first. I take the thawed chicken that I'd removed from the freezer this morning before leaving for work from the refrigerator to clean and to season it before putting it in the oven to bake, and then I put a couple of cups of rice and vegetables into the rice cooker. This will be the first time that Michael, Nicole and I will spend the weekend together which is a pretty significant milestone for our family.

We had agreed at our family meeting last week that special occasions would be considered neutral weekends where Michael would have to find separate sleeping arrangements to keep the time issues fair and so no one gets upset thinking that he's spending more time with one of us than he is with the other. This weekend, for Gabey's birthday, is our first neutral weekend so Michael will be sleeping on the couch, and Nicole will be sleeping on the futon in the third bedroom that we converted into an office/study.

Satisfied that dinner is good to go and will be ready on time, I peek over the breakfast bar to check on Gabriel. He has finished eating his cookies and is quietly building with his Legos, so I tiptoe out the back door to take one last look around in the yard.

My mom was able to borrow some tables and chairs from her job, and my dad and my brother James had brought everything over yesterday. Three long tables are set up around the perimeter of the yard and pushed back against the fence, and the folding chairs are stacked up against the side of the house. Now all we have to do is put down the tablecloths and decorations in the morning, and Michael is tasked with tying the piñata to one of the low branches of the Maple tree in the right corner of the yard.

I go back inside the house, smiling and excited about tomorrow, and thinking about the past two years. Two years ago, at this time I was a newlywed at 21 years old and about to give birth to another human being – needless to say, I was terrified. But I had gotten through it, I'd grown through it and from it, and I'd set myself to the task of being a good mother and a good wife. I pray that my efforts have been accepted, and I thank Allah for the peace and for the blessings that I've received, then and since.

I cross the kitchen and find Gabriel fast asleep on the rug in the living room with Oreo crumbs on his face and a sea of multi-colored Lego blocks around him. I turn off the t.v. and pick him up to carry him upstairs to his bedroom. His bedroom is the only room in the whole house that doesn't contain any boxes in it and that was completely arranged and organized the first night of sleeping in the house. My parents had insisted upon getting him a big boy bed so although I lay him in his crib, a twin bed is pushed against the opposite wall. The entire room is swathed in varying shades of blue, green and yellow, and it's crowded with toys and books. I look down at his sleeping features and smile, smoothing his hair away from his forehead and kissing his cheek before leaving the room with the door open and going next door to my bedroom.

I call it my bedroom because although Michael keeps some of his things here, most of his belongings are in his apartment in Boston. I cherish the signs of him in the room, well, the good ones like his books and his empty coffee cup; not the not-so-good-ones like his discarded socks or potato chip crumbs in the bed. Today the only sign of him is a kufi that he left on the dresser and his bath towel strewn over the back of the armchair near the closet. I tuck his kufi into the top right hand dresser drawer containing his socks and his other kufis then I toss his towel into the hamper in the adjoining master bathroom.

I change out of my work clothes and into one of my favorite kaftans, a white cotton with multi-colored flowers printed in purple, turquoise and dark green on it, and I brush my hair up into a loose bun on the top of my head. I put my discarded work clothes into the hamper and then go downstairs on bare feet to check on dinner.

The rice and vegetables are done so I turn off the rice cooker and transfer the rice and veggies into a rectangular glass pan and cover it with aluminum foil to keep it warm, but the chicken is still cooking. I tidy up the living room, wash the few dishes that remain in the kitchen sink, and go back upstairs, peeking into Gabriel's room on the way to make sure that he's still sleeping, and go back to my bedroom to unpack the rest of the boxes in there.

There are four boxes left: one box of shoes, a box of sweaters to hang up in the closet, a box of mail (mostly bills) and paperwork from college, and a box of mementos and personal stuff that I've saved from over the years. Feeling nostalgic, I walk over to the box of mementos near the bureau and drag it over to the bookshelf by the bed.

When I open the box the first thing on top is Gabriel's baby book from his first year of life. I leaf through it leisurely, smiling at the photos, and getting weepy while reading the gushingly overzealous new mom entries about when he first said mama and dada, and when he took his first steps. I finally get to the end and slide it onto the empty bookshelf before reaching into the box for the photo albums from high school and college.

I look through every page of my high school album first, laughing out loud at some of the pictures and sitting quietly, thoughtfully reflecting about others. The smiling image of my younger self wearing her cap and gown at her high school graduation stares back at me, encouraging me to remember and to never forget the magic of that time. I wipe away tears as I close that album and slide it onto the bookshelf beside Gaby's baby book.

Then I open to the first few pictures of my college album, which have me grinning from ear to ear, re-experiencing the raw joy of those moments. The captured memories pull me back to those days of unrestrained exhilaration and a pure love for life. Everything had a shine to it back then, even daily tasks like eating and going to class. I get stuck at a picture of Michael.

He's at a table in one of the university libraries with an open book in front of him and a stack of books at his elbow, and he gazes out from the image with a look of surprise on his face. I clearly remember that day and how Nicole and I and a couple of other friends had noticed him sitting there on our way out of the library. He and I weren't dating at the time, but I knew that there was something about him that I was attracted to, and I loved his smile and the way his eyes got squinty when he laughed so I had said, "hey!" and had snapped a picture when he had looked up. I sit wondering what he might have been thinking about that day when I hear the front door open downstairs.

I had been so caught up in my thoughts that I hadn't even heard his car pull into the driveway below the bedroom window.

"As salaamu alaikum!" I hear him call out as he enters the house.

I close the album, put it onto the shelf next the other one, and push the cardboard box against the wall before standing up and going downstairs.

Michael is putting the large, gift wrapped box containing Gabriel's tricycle onto the floor when I get to the bottom of the stairs, and Nicole is standing by the door holding an open cardboard box full of little plastic loot bags containing toys and candy from the Dollar Store. This is her first time to the house, so she's looking around and smiling.

"Wasalaamu alaikum," I say when I reach the bottom of the stairs.

We're all still getting used to feeling comfortable showing affection around each other, so the hugs are awkward, but genuine as we attempt to make each other feel comfortable and welcome.

"I love the house!" Nicole says enthusiastically as she hands me the box of loot bags.

"Me too! Isn't it cute!" I respond as I carry the box into the kitchen. "I've almost finished unpacking everything. I'll show you where the study is upstairs so you can put your bag down and get comfortable, and then hopefully we can take a little tour before dinner."

"Ok," she replies and takes off her jacket.

Michael reaches for it to hang it up onto one of the hooks by the door before taking off his own jacket and hanging it up too. She and I pass the small musalla on the right side of the front of the house, opposite the living room, and her eyes brighten at the sight of the tidy prayer space and soft lighting. She has a similar area in her apartment, and she had suggested some of the touches that I had made to ours. We exchange a shared look of happiness as she follows me upstairs.

"I love that!" she gushes and squeezes my arm affectionately.

"I hoped you would! You were so right about the candles, and I got the last set of matching prayer rugs from the Islamic store," I reply.

"Love it, love it, love it!" she says as we reach the top of the stairs.

"This is Gabriel's room," I say as we peek into the room. "He's napping but should be up soon."

"So sweet!" she says as she looks around. "Your mom insisted on that bed, huh?"

We laugh quietly, and I reply, "Of course she did. And dad backed her up so, we have a twin bed. I guess Michael can sleep in here if he doesn't want to sleep on the couch, but the couch will probably be more comfortable."

We laugh again, imagining Michael on the twin bed, and walk toward my bedroom, right next door to Gabey's, and then the bathroom across the hall from my room before we reach the study at the end of the hall.

"Everything looks so nice!" she says and walks over to the windows in the study that overlook the front yard of the house and the driveway. "You've done a great job with the decorating."

"Most of the stuff in here was given to us from my uncle, except for the bookshelves, Imam Yasir gave those to us. And the futon folds out to a full-size mattress so you should have plenty of room," I say, happy that she likes the house and the touches I've made to it.

"I'm sure it will be comfortable," Nicole says and puts her overnight bag onto the armchair by the door.

"Somebody is awake," Michael says and enters the study carrying Gabriel in his arms.

"Dada home," Gabriel announces to us, his two-year-old voice is thick with sleep as he pats Michael's chest affectionately.

"Yes, Dada's home! And Auntie Niki is here too," I reply.

Gabriel leans forward and reaches happily for Nicole in response and Michael hands him over to her.

"As Salaamu Alaikum, my big boy," Nicole says and kisses Gabey's cheeks. "You're getting so big! And talking so well! How are you?"

"Slaam alikum," Gabriel replies and wraps his arms around Nicole's neck. "Gabey hungry. Ca' have some cookies?"

One of his new quirks is referring to himself in the third person. We laugh and Nicole looks over at me before responding.

"Gabey hungry? Ok, let's ask mommy?" she says and hands him to me.

"No cookies, but you can have some dinner," I say and hug him close as I step towards the doorway.

"Dada hungry too," Michael says, and we laugh again as we leave the study and head downstairs.

"The chicken should be done by now, and the rice and vegetables are already cooked so we can all eat-eat," I reply mainly to Gabey but to Michael and Nicole too.

I hand Gabriel back to Michael when we reach the bottom of the stairs and I walk into the kitchen to open the oven. The baked chicken is golden brown and simmering in its own juices, and the fragrant smell of oregano, garlic and basil fills my nostrils as I remove the glass pan and place it onto the counter.

"It's ready," I announce.

"Smells delicious," Nicole says.

"Let's eat-eat," Michael states eagerly and Gabey claps his hands and copies him.

"Yea. Eat-eat!" Gabriel says excitedly.

Michael carries him into the dining room and puts him into the chair at the table containing his booster seat then straps him in as I show Nicole where the plates and cups are kept so she can set the table while I bring out the food. She and I move comfortably around the kitchen with each other as if we have been doing it for years, and I offer a silent prayer of thanks to Allah for the ease and peace between us.

Once everything is on the table, we all sit down and smile at each other. This is our first dinner together as a family unit and the milestone upfront in our minds. Michael grins happily, and infectiously, and my heart swells with affection for him. Without words, all three of us recognize the progress we've made and we bow our heads to say grace.

"Oh, Allah, we thank you for this food that we are about to receive, and for all of your many blessings, Amin," Michael says.

"Amin," Nicole and I repeat in unison.

"Aah-meen," Gabey says belatedly and Michael playfully ruffles the curls of his hair in response.

I serve Gabey some rice and broccoli then start cutting his chicken into bite sized pieces as Michael and Nicole serve themselves.

"The chicken looks good, just how I like it," Michael says as he dishes two large chicken thighs from the pan and puts them onto his plate.

"Smells good too," Nicole says as he hands her the serving fork for the chicken. "You have to tell me how you seasoned it, Jo. Is that basil?"

"Yes. Basil and Oregano," I tell her as I finish with Gabey and start filling my own plate. "And some garlic, four cloves, some paprika, half an onion, a little chicken bullion, and some ground black pepper."

We eat in a comfortable silence, making conversation here in there about the work week and the expected weather for the weekend, and it feels like home. After dinner I bring Gabey upstairs to put him to sleep while Michael and Nicole clean up and put the leftovers away. Gabriel falls asleep easily when I play the Quran recitation for him on the small CD player in his bedroom and I make it back downstairs for in time for prayer.

The three of us line up together, and as I stand beside Nicole, shoulder to shoulder, and toe to toe, my eyes prick with tears of gratitude, and I thank Allah for His Grace and for the blessing of being permitted to witness a love like this.

La ilaha illalaah. There is no god but God.

Glossary

Abaya: a loose, robe-like dress worn by many Muslim women

Al hamdulilah: an Arabic phrase of praise meaning All Praise is to Allah (God)

Allah: the Arabic word for God

As salaamu alaikum: The Muslim greeting commonly translated as meaning peace be upon you

Asr: The middle afternoon required Islamic salaat prayer

Dawah: the act of inviting people to embrace, or convert to, Islam

Deen: the way of life of Muslim believers which complies with the divine laws, beliefs and deeds associated with the Islamic religion

Dua: Prayer supplications; can be made at any time of the day and does not require the ritual cleansing of Wudu to be offered

Fajr: The pre-dawn required Islamic salaat prayer

Fard: that which is required by Islamic law according to the religion of Islam

Hadeeth: teachings of the sayings and sunnah of the Prophet Muhammad (may peace be upon him)

Imam: the title of the religious leader of the mosque/masjid in the Islamic religion

Isha: the nightly required Islamic salaat prayer

Istikharah: a prayer recited by Muslims when seeking guidance from Allah when facing a decision in their life.

Jumuah: The Friday congregational prayer at the Masjid/Mosque practiced by Muslims

Kufi: a brimless, short, rounded cap worn by some Muslim men and among many populations in Africa and Southern Asia

La ilaha illaalaah: the transliteration of the Arabic Islamic phrase meaning there is no god but God

Masjid/Mosque: consecrated prayer space for worship in the Islamic community

Mumu: a loose-fitting dress, usually sewn from one large piece of fabric, that is worn by many Muslim women

Musalla: informal prayer space outside of a masjid/mosque

Nation of Islam: an Islamic organization founded by Elijah Muhammad and based within the U.S. that teaches doctrine that isn't taught or subscribed to by traditional Muslims

Qari: a person in the Islamic tradition who recites the Quran with the proper rules of recitation

Quran: The holy revelation of the Islamic religion as revealed to the Prophet Muhammad (peace be upon him) by the Archangel Gabriel 1400 years ago

Rakaats: a cycle of prescribed movements and prayers that are performed in the ritual Islamic salaat

Salaams: a casual term referring to greeting someone with the Islamic greeting of peace

Salaat: The required ritual Islamic prayer taught by the Prophet Muhammad (may peace be upon him) to be prayed at five specific times daily by all Muslims; Fajr, Zuhr, Asr, Maghrib, and Isha

Shahadah: One of the major tenets of belief in Islam and the Muslim declaration of faith; La ilaha ilalah (There is no God but Allah)

Surahs: the Arabic word loosely translated to mean chapters which refers to the chapters of the Quran

Taqwa: an Islamic term for being conscious and cognizant of God, of truth and of piety

Walaikum as salaam/Wasalaamu alaikum: The Muslim response to the greeting of As Salaamu Alaikum and commonly translated as meaning and peace be returned to you

Wudu: The ritual cleansing for the Islamic ritual salaat prayer

One Love, Two Wives

Music Playlist

Chapter One, Springtime: Closer – Goapele

Chapter Two, The Announcement: Goodbye – Alicia Keys

Chapter Three, The Aftermath: Bag Lady – Erykah Badu

Chapter Four, What?!: Ifuleave – Musiq Soulchild & Mary J. Blige

Chapter Five, Istikharah: Don't You Forget It – Glenn Lewis

Chapter Six, Coming to Terms: Best Part – H.E.R. & Daniel Caesar

Chapter Seven, Woman to Woman: Just Fine – Mary J. Blige

Chapter Eight, Girlfriends: Count On Me – CeCe Winans & Whitney Houston

Chapter Nine, Daddy's Girl: Daddy - Beyonce

Chapter Ten, Her: Orange Moon – Erykah Badu

Chapter Eleven, Him: Unbreakable – Alicia Keys

Chapter Twelve, Us: Spend My Life With You – Eric Benet

Chapter Thirteen, Autumn: Before I Let Go – Frankie Beverly & Maze

About the Author

Janette Grant is a freelance writer and author. She is also the Executive Editor of Mindworks Publishing, a desktop publishing company specializing in the production of books that build interfaith bridges for promoting understanding and tolerance between cultures.

Janette converted to Islam from Christianity in her youth, and she has a deep personal interest in interfaith discussions. She writes poetry in her free time and she currently resides outside of Houston, Texas with her family.

You can follow her on social media by searching:

Mindworks Publishing on Facebook

Author Janette Grant on Facebook and Amazon Books